# 4 SLEUTHS & A BACHELORETTE

## A KILLER FOURSOME MYSTERY

LESLIE LANGTRY     ARLENE MCFARLANE

TRACI ANDRIGHETTI     DIANA ORGAIN

4 SLEUTHS & A BACHELORETTE

A Killer Foursome Mystery

ebook ISBN-13: 978-1-9994981-6-0
print ISBN: 978-1-9994981-7-7

Published by LMAO Press
Canada

Cover Design by Arlene McFarlane
Cover by Adrian Doan Kim

Formatting by Traci Andrighetti

❀ Created with Vellum

# VALENTINE

## ARLENE MCFARLANE

"Who's Babette Lang?" Max Martell, my wingman in the salon and occasional worrywart, flipped the invitation back and forth in his hand. "And why is this"—he read the name on the RSVP again—"Merry Wrath inviting you to Babette's bachelorette party?"

It was seven-thirty, Saturday morning, middle of June. Max had agreed to come into work before my two other employees to go over final details before I left for a weekend at Niagara Falls. Naturally, he was more interested in learning about Babette than talking details that were already fixed in his clever brain. He practically stepped on my sparkly heels as I traipsed from my office to my station, stuffing last-minute supplies into my black beauty bag.

I wasn't trying to put him off, but I had other things on my mind. Top of the list: why *was* I invited to Babette's bachelorette party? She'd sworn off men three years ago after Greasy Toes Ricco had persuaded her *then* slimy fiancé to jump off the Brooklyn Bridge with a cement block tied to his ankle. Lucky Babette, escaping *that* marriage! Unfortunately, I hadn't seen her since that bachelorette party.

"Val-en-*tine!*"

I ceased from shoving my flat iron into my bag and gave Max a tolerant look, making this as succinct as I could. "Babette is one of my best friends." At least she was during our childhood. "Merry must be another friend who was in charge of sending out invitations to the party. It's as simple as that."

Max puckered his lips, telling me it wasn't that simple. "I thought *I* was your best friend."

Oh Lord. If I had to explain this one more time I'd take my scissors and stab myself in the temple. We weren't teenagers anymore, and it seemed silly talking in terms of best friends. But for Max's sake, I smiled and put on the voice I saved for kids when I cut their hair.

"You already know Twix was my best friend from ballet class. But before I'd met Twix, there was Babette." I grinned at the memory of playing with my chubby, blonde friend, a year my senior. "We were inseparable. We lived two doors away from each other and were always getting into our moms' makeup and jewelry. But that was then, and this is now. And *you*, my dear, handsome, gifted stylist, are my adult, *male* best friend." Unlike a perm, flattery could never be over-processed.

Max narrowed his hazel eyes at me in suspicion, but my words must have touched a soft spot since the glum shadow on his face brightened, stopping him from grilling me further. Good thing, too. I was already late and didn't want to miss my morning flight.

I inhaled the smells of hairspray and bleach that always hung in the air and took a final glance around Beaumont's, making sure everything was in order. I'd made the mistake of leaving the shop for short periods before, and fortunately the walls were still standing when I'd returned.

Maybe I was being paranoid, but Beaumont's was mine, from its rustic Mediterranean charm to the twinkling lights and stucco walls. The airy European theme didn't exactly cry small-town

Rueland, Massachusetts, but that was okay. It spoke to my French and Armenian heritage, which felt more fitting.

I slipped a quick kiss on Max's fashionably stubbly cheek and looked up in silent prayer that everything would be fine while I was gone. Then I picked up an apple fritter from Friar Tuck's bakery next door to eat on the road and jumped in my yellow Bug for Boston Logan Airport.

I veered out of the parking lot, patted for my beauty bag beside me, and screeched to a stop, smacking my hand on the dashboard before I flew through the windshield. Where was my trusty black bag?

I wrenched around and inspected the backseat. *Whew.* I was so rattled this morning, I didn't realize I'd thrown it in the back beside Babette's gift.

To be honest, I didn't go anywhere without my beauty bag. This hadn't always been the case. It all happened that infamous day when I'd nabbed a killer with a perm rod and a lot of pluck. It wasn't one of my finer moments on account of the unsavory spot where I clamped the perm rod, but suddenly I became the world's first beautician to catch crooks using her beauty tools.

Contrary to popular belief, I'm not Wonder Woman, and I'm not as kickass as Lara Croft: Tomb Raider, even if we have the same hair. I'm a petite 5'4", I have an eye for fashion, and people tell me I have exotic looks. In other words, I'm the last person anyone would suspect of apprehending a killer.

When I'm lucky enough to snag one, more often than not, it catches them by surprise. Ironically, it catches me by surprise, too. Truth is, I go from being in supreme control to questioning my moves and acting on impulse. Still, I learned long ago, never underestimate the many uses of a simple flat iron or razor. I had no plans this weekend of using my tools as weapons, but old habits die hard.

No sooner had I stepped off the plane in sunny Buffalo when my cell phone buzzed. *Max.*

I'd planned to get in some sightseeing and shopping, but instead I was being shuffled for the third time around the baggage claim, the pink boa I'd used as wrapping for Babette's gift unraveling with each step. Amid being pushed and shoved by a hundred other passengers, some kid spilled grape juice in front of me, almost causing me to slip and break my neck. I like kids, but *eek!*

"What!" I was hungry and at my limit and didn't mean to bark into the phone at Max. On top of everything else, my suitcase with all the party decorations hadn't made it to Buffalo.

Max made a nervous peep. "Wanted to let you know everything is running smoothly." Code for *All hell's breaking loose.*

"What's going on, Max? Where are you?"

"Since you asked, I'm in your office, hiding." The *creak* I heard was confirmation he'd plopped onto my office chair. I could almost smell his heavenly cologne filling the room.

"From what?"

"What do you think? Miss Cuckoo, a.k.a. Phyllis Murdoch, strikes again."

Phyllis is my second employee and couldn't cut a straight bang if she had a two-by-four nailed to her client's head. I'd tried to let her go in the past, but she's a distant relative, and, well, guilt is an intricate thing when it comes to firing a family member.

I click-clacked over to the claims-counter line, dragging my suitcase and Babette's gift behind me. "I'm afraid to ask. What'd Phyllis do now?"

"She's re-perming one side of Mrs. Horowitz's head."

"Mrs. Horowitz?" Oh boy. God Himself wouldn't be able to please that woman or take the wigged look out of her hair. Now

Phyllis was working on her? Mrs. Horowitz also never made appointments. Figured she'd pick today to drop in and ask for a perm. "What are you talking about? Didn't the perm take?"

"It took on *one* side. But Phyllis ran out of perm solution and had to open another bottle."

Great. Not only was Phyllis starting the day running my business into the ground, but she was driving me into the red along the way. "What happened?"

"She snipped the perm bottle and, before she finished applying the solution, a daddy long-legs danced across the perm-rod tray, scaring the bejeebers out of her." He chuckled to himself. "Naturally, Phyllis screamed like a banshee, squirting the spider and everything else in a ten-foot radius."

"An-n-nd?" I rubbed my forehead, praying the hammering behind my eyes wasn't the start of a headache.

"The shop's a disaster, but the good news is the spider curled up all six legs and quit dancing."

I didn't want to split hairs because heaven knows I had enough on my mind, but I couldn't let this detail go. "Eight, not six."

Silence filtered through the line. "Eight not six, what?"

"Legs. Spiders have eight legs."

I heard him sigh into the phone. "After Phyllis squirted the spider and its *eight* legs, there wasn't enough solution left for Mrs. Horowitz's hair. I told her as much, but did she listen?"

A man behind the claims counter motioned me forward. "Max, I have to go."

"Fine. If you don't hear from me again, you know it's because I've strangled Phyllis." He paused dramatically. "Or maybe I'll let Jock handle her."

At the mention of my third employee's name, a shot of heat soared through me. Jock was ex-navy, an extraordinary stylist, and a constant mystery. He was also a combination of Hercules,

Superman, and Thor. On top of that, he was God's gift to women. If *he* couldn't handle Phyllis and salvage Mrs. Horowitz's hair, no one could.

"*Lady*," the claims guy urged, waving me on.

I snapped out of it, swallowing dryly. "Just don't burn down the place while I'm gone," I said to Max, then hung up.

AFTER WASTING two more hours at the airport, waiting for the claims department to locate my party bag, I was promised that the airline would do its best delivering it to the hotel by tonight. With everything else that had gone wrong, I wasn't holding my breath.

I dropped off my stuff in my room by mid-afternoon and made a mental note of the things I needed to do. First was food. My rumbling stomach reminded me I hadn't eaten since the donut this morning.

Next, I wanted to give Babette a hug and wish her congratulations in person on her upcoming marriage to Charlie. After a quick hello, I'd pick up the cake—my personal contribution for the bachelorette party. And, gee, if I were lucky, maybe I'd find some last-minute decorations. I could do everything at Higgly Piggly, the local grocery store where Babette worked.

I hopped in a cab, thinking how fortunate it was that Merry Wrath, the guest-list lady, gave me Kate Connolly's name, the friend handling the food. Kate was thrilled at my offer to look after the cake. Sounded like she already had enough on her plate.

The cabbie chewed on his unlit cigar, playing tour guide as we passed one seedy hotel after another. "You ain't gonna see much of the Falls staying at the Park Avenue Hotel or what we locals call the Park Avenue Dump. Girl like you should be staying at the Ritz. Or at least closer to the Falls."

I smiled at his fatherly eyes glancing back at me in the rearview mirror. "I'm actually here for a bachelorette party."

I'd caught a glimpse of the beautiful Falls earlier and understood why the landmark was the honeymoon capital of the world. But why have the bachelorette party here? And why was Babette working at a grocery store instead of the pharmaceutical company where she'd been?

"Bachelorette party, huh? Better be careful." He swerved into Higgly Piggly's parking lot. "Those parties can get out of hand, what with all the booze and goings-on."

Ha. This was one girl who wouldn't be drinking. I gave him a tip, thanked him for the ride, and jumped out of the cab before he could give me any more advice.

I pulled out my invitation that I'd snatched back from Max once he'd finished raking me over the coals and double-checked the party started at eight. Lots of time to get my jobs done.

I stuffed the invite back in my bag and took a huge, calming breath. I got here in one piece, the sky wasn't falling—I looked up —yet, anyway, and the rest of the weekend would go off without a hitch. The tension eased from my shoulders, and my nervous insides relaxed. Yes. Everything was going to be fine.

Higgly Piggly was a large, clean food market, but it had seen better days. I wandered the aisles, keeping an eye open for Babette amidst the distant drilling, pounding, and other sounds of refurbishing in the store.

Butterflies tickled my stomach and instant memories flooded me of the fun we'd had dressing in our moms' old gowns and pretending to be movie stars. Babette was not a shy child. She had no qualms, squashing her tubby body into a gown, prancing around the neighborhood, acting like her favorite star of all time, Marilyn Monroe.

Babette always did have a flamboyant side and a voice as smooth as silk. If anyone was going to make it to Hollywood, she was the one. Of course, once she moved to the other side of Boston at age twelve, and then to California a few years later, communication with one another had been sporadic. Far as I knew, she'd never gotten a crack at becoming an actress.

I turned the corner into the deli section and approached the sandwich counter for something to eat when I was distracted by a weird figure, twenty feet away, dressed as a tall rubbery foam hot dog, dancing a jig in goofy hot dog shoes while handing shoppers mini sausages on toothpicks.

The wiener curved like a banana a foot above the guy's head and had a yellow squiggly line down the front. There wasn't a lot of oomph in his step, but every time someone took a sample on a toothpick, he stuffed a tiny glass jar of mustard in their bag, then gave a hearty wave as if trying to make the best out of a sorry situation.

My mouth watered at the smell of the mini sausages. They looked good, too. Plump and juicy with those tiny dabs of mustard on top. I sidestepped closer, avoiding eye contact with the human hot dog, wanting to grab a sample without drawing attention to myself or being danced to.

I was within two feet when he started singing the company's wiener ditty. Wait a minute! That wasn't a guy's voice. Even with the drilling in the background, I could tell that lustrous voice belonged to a female. *Holy jumpin'!* Not just any female. That was Babette's voice.

I twirled around and stared into the face of my once chubby friend, her tall, voluptuous figure hidden inside the foam costume, her eyelids sparkling with eyeshadow the color of yellow and green condiments. It wasn't meant to look garish, but as a beautician, I would've toned it down a bit.

"Babette?"

Her eyes widened. "Valentine!" Ignoring ogles from shoppers, she dropped the tray on the table beside her and pulled me in for a warm squeeze.

I gaped wordlessly past her shoulder, then back at her in her hot dog costume. "Why are you dressed as a wiener?" Oops. I really had to work on my quick tongue.

She picked up the tray again, offering me a sample, and filled me in on her job situation. "It's not all bad," she cooed, her mouth twitching into a thin grin. "I get these complimentary baby jars of mustards that my boss, Stanley, wants to charge customers for." She pried open my bag with her free hand and tossed some inside. "*Tightwad.* He'd kill me if he saw me handing these out."

She bit her luscious lips, and suddenly I was back to hot summer days, eating red Popsicles as kids, then giggling as Babette chased neighborhood boys for a fat kiss.

I bit into a mini sausage, and she smiled, trying to make light of things. "I even got a commercial spot dressed in this wienie."

I gulped down the bite that seemed to stick in my throat. "Well, that's...something." I wanted to be encouraging, but what more was there to say when my friend was dressed like the Oscar Mayer wiener?

"Of course, Stanley negotiated a deal with my agent, ensuring he sat in on the whole production." She rolled her eyes coolly, then slid the tray back on the table. "Cheapskate."

Yikes. This was worse than I thought. How could Babette have sunk so low?

"Enough about me." She pushed her face through the rubber hole to take a better look at me. "You look gorgeous as ever! Little Valentine, with her long, glossy hair, always made up adorably." She grabbed my hands and held me out at arm's length. "And here you are, dressed in pink, cute tutu and all."

This was just like Babette. She didn't see things through dull lenses. In her eyes, I was a ballerina with enough sparkle to light up a room. I looked down at myself. In truth, my sleeveless dress and light-to-dark pink skirt *did* have a sheer tutu effect. And okay, my glittery hoop earrings and spiked heels didn't hurt the look. But Babette simply had a way of making you feel good about yourself.

A guy hauling a beer belly ambled up to us and gawked from the tray of wieners to Babette. "You work here? Or is someone else handing those out?"

Unruffled by his ignorance, Babette looked the guy square on, her voice laced with sarcasm. "Someone else is handing them out. He's in the frozen food section dressed as a Fudgsicle."

The guy grunted and hoisted up his pants. "Figures I'd get *this kind* of service *here*."

"Awful, isn't it?" Her smile was unapologetic. "If I were you, I'd hit the grocery store down the street. Tell them I sent you."

The guy trucked off, and Babette's face instantly lit up as if we hadn't been interrupted. "Tell me all about that swarthy, tough detective you're wildly in love with. I hear he's hard-muscled and *hot*."

I loved that our moms kept up with the finer details of our lives from the old neighborhood. Wouldn't want to miss a chance at friendly gossip.

"*Ooh*, Michael Romero," she gushed. "Even his name sounds sexy."

I understood the sentiment. My breath caught in my throat at the mention of Romero's name, sparking the memory of his intimate send-off when I'd told him I was going away for the weekend. But Babette was engaged, and this was all in fun. Or was it? Her words were sincere, and her eyelids were full of sparkle, yet she'd lost some sparkle, and the slight nervousness in her tone told me something was worrying her. Might've been her tightwad boss. Maybe it was her job.

*Oh no.* My pulse stopped cold in my veins. What if it was Charlie and her upcoming marriage? I hadn't met *this* fiancé, but the last one was no prize. Babette didn't have the greatest track record when it came to men, and I hoped, if she was taking the plunge again, that this time she was certain.

"We'll catch up at the party." I wolfed down another wiener and gave her a quick hug.

"Okay, but Valentine…please don't announce it that I work here. I mean, most of you know, but I'd rather not publicize that I'm wearing this dreadful costume day in and day out."

I might've screwed up on the decorations, and I might've ruined the wrapping on her gift, and I might've—wait. Where was I going with all this? Oh yeah. I could do this favor for Babette. "My lips are sealed. Just don't forget to act surprised when you arrive later."

She gave me a strange look. "Huh? I already know about the party."

"I know, but it'll be more fun when you walk in if you act shocked."

She swung her hips back and forth in a seductive way. "If there's one thing I can do, it's act."

IT WAS ALMOST SIX O'CLOCK, and the front desk had heard nothing from the airline about my bag. This meant I needed to get creative on how I was going to beautify the party room.

The hotel assured me they had white tablecloths—a plus—and tall candleholders if I needed them. I had balloons I'd picked up at the grocery store. They had Dora the Explorer's face on them, but it was either that or Bart Simpson's thanks to Higgly Piggly's noisy party section being under renovation, leaving me little choice. At any rate, Dora was a kickass little adventurer like Babette always was. And the balloons had a pink background. Good enough for me.

The other small issue was the cake. The bakery's decorator had gone home sick, and I didn't get the cake I'd ordered. Well, I promised a cake for this party, and a cake was what I got.

I returned to the matter at hand and dumped the contents of

my beauty bag onto the bed, taking stock of what I had. Combs. Scissors. Flat iron. Bobby pins. Nail polish. Ribbons. Hair extensions? Hmm. I'd planned on taking those out after Monday's playtime visit with the hospital sick kids. I grinned. Cute tykes, even if I did walk out of Rueland Memorial half the time with nail stickers on my nose and lipstick on my cheeks.

I steered my gaze from my black bag to the flashy, hot pink shoulder bag I'd bought as Babette's bachelorette gift. Unfortunately, the shimmery pink boa that once covered it was in a heap on the bed. Well, decorating the bag with it was a good idea at the time.

I went back to studying the hair extensions. They weren't fabulous on their own, but if I had skewers to give them a spine, then stuck a wisp of boa down the middle and pinned a few glittery bobby pins on the hair ends, they might make attractive, cascading centerpieces. And at the end of the night, each guest could take home a handful of posh bobby pins. I rounded up little tubs of butterscotch conditioner that had also been floating around in my bag. Perfect. Another party favor.

Heck, Babette wouldn't care if her gift wasn't wrapped. More, she'd go gaga over the contents inside: massage oils, bubble bath, sexy slippers, mini bottle of champagne, and bag of red jelly beans—her favorite. To spruce it up, I staged the bag open and tied a ribbon through the straps into a fancy bow. It had Valentine panache, and Babette would love it.

THE PARTY ROOM had an honest-to-god funeral-parlor feel. A fake fireplace leaned against one wall, abstract pictures hung on another, and functional drapes decked the windows. Mr. Clean could've done wonders with the stale smoke in the air, but at least the tablecloths looked clean, and the Dora the Explorer balloons brightened the place.

Good thing I'd given myself a squirt of my signature Musk perfume before leaving my room. I would've had to shoot myself if the smell of stale smoke followed me around all night.

I glanced at the buffet table where a female a few years older than I am in a light, baggy top and dark pants inspected trays of finger foods. She had mid-length brown hair bordering on frizzy, and from the back it looked like she was counting things off on her fingers. By her appearance, I guessed she was the caterer.

I zoomed in on the table. Aha! Fruit kabobs with bamboo skewers! Exactly what I needed for my centerpieces. I could almost hear the *Mission Impossible* music as I plotted how to pinch the skewers from the fruit tray without attracting attention.

I almost had my execution drilled in my head when the woman at the table turned slightly and licked her lips. She was quite adorable with big round eyes, and *yowza*, she was pregnant, *really* pregnant. Maybe she was having one of those pregnant-woman cravings I always heard about. But *was* she the caterer? An employee? A guest?

She turned back to the table, leaned over, and popped a cream puff in her mouth. No way! Now I *knew* she wasn't an employee. Granted, this wasn't the Ritz. If a worker filched a cream puff, who cared? Not me. I wasn't here to snitch. I was focused on the fruit kabobs.

I took a cursory glance around the room to see what else was happening. A slim woman with short, curly blonde hair gave a casual look at the clipboard in her hand, then shrugged and exited the room. Merry Wrath perhaps?

The bartender was busy talking to an older woman sitting at the bar who was wearing a wig that looked on par with Mrs. Horowitz's hair. She was sampling—or more like slugging—a serious glass of alcohol. I envied her. One glass of that stuff and I'd be flat out on the floor for the rest of the evening. Exactly why I wouldn't be drinking tonight.

My gaze shifted back to the pregnant woman. Poor thing. Her

unmanageable curly hair looked like it could use some TLC. Maybe once she was done popping cream puffs, I'd go over and hand her a few tubs of butterscotch conditioner. While I waited for her to vacate the food table, I plunked the fancied hair extensions into the tall candleholders that the staff had provided.

My insides bubbled with delight at the array. Forget the skewers. The glittery extensions flared up from the candleholders and cascaded out like fountains. It was a sight to behold!

I was about to pat myself on the back when the pregnant woman dusted the icing sugar from her hands, gave me a short wave, and waddled over. I turned around, wondering if she was looking at someone else, but there was no one behind me. Only the cake that I was hiding.

She stopped in front of me and extended her hand. "Valentine?"

"Yes?" I smiled and shook her hand.

"Kate Connolly. I'm a friend of Babette's. I saw you decorating, and from everything Babette's said about you, I knew this had to be Valentine."

I wanted to ask if *everything* meant acting on instinct, getting into trouble, and regretting my mistakes, like purchasing the hunk of pastry behind me. Instead, I gave a faint, lighthearted laugh, curbing my nose from twitching like it always did when I was nervous or in danger.

"Thanks for handling the cake." She peered over my shoulder. "Is that it?"

"Uh, yes."

"Awesome. Would you mind if we put it on the buffet table with the rest of the food?"

I bit my lip, harried by the memory of what I'd gone through today. "Sure."

I moved aside, and Kate looked down at the cake. "It says *Happy Birthday Harry*."

"I know. Do you think Babette will notice?"

Kate giggled, then shifted her stare from the cake, to the funeral-parlor setting, to the motley crew that were beginning to arrive, and I knew she was wondering what else was in store for tonight.

# KATE

## DIANA ORGAIN

 **o Do:**

1. Figure out food for Babette's bachelorette party.
2. Call home.
3. See Niagara Falls.
4. Try not to miss Laurie and Jim too much.
5. Does this hotel have a spa?

"Would you mind excusing me for a second?" I asked Valentine. "My feet are killing me." I rubbed my protruding belly.

*Being six months pregnant with twins is no walk in the park.*

"I think I have a few minutes before Babette gets here. Plus, I'm dying to call home," I said.

"Of course," Valentine said. "Don't give it a second thought. I'll put the cake on the table with the rest of the food."

I nodded my thanks and wiggled my fingers at her, then turned and crossed the dank party room. Seriously, the hotel needed a little TLC.

*What had Babette been thinking?*

Maybe she didn't know how rundown the hotel had become. My invitation had come from a Merry Wrath, whom I hadn't met yet. Probably the party was a surprise to Babette.

But she'd smile and play along. Babette was a trouper.

I was excited to see her. We'd been friends since college, and I hadn't seen her since my own bachelorette party, which my best friend Paula had arranged on a Napa Valley Wine Train tour. But my poor feet had swelled on the plane and I needed to get them propped up stat, or I'd be reduced to wearing the non-slip socks they'd given me during the flight.

I passed the fake fireplace and left the room. At the end of the hotel corridor, a heavy exit door was propped open. Mercifully, gales of crisp air streamed in. I gulped greedily, thankful to breathe air that was fresher than in the party room. I marched toward the elevator just as a harried woman reeking of cigarette smoke and screaming on her cell phone burst through the exit door and closed it.

"She's no good! I keep telling ya that. Why don't you listen for once in your life?" she shrieked into her mobile.

I pressed the elevator button and waited, trying not to eavesdrop.

"Listen, everyone wants their big break. They just don't want to work for it." She squinted over at me, her eyeliner and mascara so heavily applied it was hard to make out if she wore false eyelashes or if there was a bat stuck to her face. She had a mop of blonde curls gathered at the top of her head and bright red lipstick stuck to her teeth.

"Going up?" she screeched at me.

I refrained from notifying her that we were on the ground level and that up was the only way to go. Instead, I politely nodded.

"Good!" she barked.

The elevator pinged and the doors opened. As much as I was desperate to get to my room, I hesitated.

*Do I really need to ride the elevator with this woman?*

She stepped into the elevator and thrust a bangled arm out to hold the door for me. I obediently followed her in.

"Don't call me, I'll call you," she cracked into the phone and abruptly hung up. She turned to me and demanded, "Floor?"

"Four," I squeaked.

She whacked the number panel. "You here for the party?"

I nodded as the elevator lurched upward.

"How do you know Babette?"

My eyes widened. How could *this woman* possibly know Babette?

"College," I mustered. "And you?"

The elevator pinged and the doors whooshed opened.

"I'm her talent agent, darling."

Talent agent? Babette was a pharmaceutical salesperson. When had she landed a talent agent?

Before I could react, she strode out of the elevator, and a couple stepped in. The woman had a severe, striking look with dark wavy hair and wore a classic navy sheath dress suit. The man looked a bit disheveled. His hair was floppy in front and, although he wore a brown blazer, his blue dress shirt was unbuttoned almost to his navel.

"You're making a mistake, Charlie," the woman said. "That's all I'm saying."

Charlie?

*Babette's groom was named Charlie...could this be the groom-to-be?*

The doors closed and the elevator jolted upward. The woman's hand flew to the side railing. "Are we going *up*?"

Charlie flashed me a look. "Sorry. We didn't check."

"No problem," I said. "Just popping up to my room before the party. Are you Charlie Miller?"

He straightened. "I am. And you are?"

The elevator pinged, having arrived on my floor. "I'm Kate Connolly, Babette's friend."

The woman's face soured at the mention of Babette.

*What was that about?*

Charlie turned to the woman. "You head on down, Chelsea. Have a good time." He held the elevator door for me and followed me out. As soon as the door closed, he sighed. "My sister is kind of high maintenance."

Hmmm. Babette's future sister-in-law was troublesome.

*Why wasn't she ecstatic to have Babette join their family?*

Anyone with half a brain would be over the moon to welcome Babette into their family. Then I thought of my own troublesome sister-in-law. Family could be challenging, especially the extended-family kind.

"Is there anything I can help you with?" Charlie asked, looking pointedly at my protruding belly.

I didn't know whether to be offended or relieved. At six months pregnant I wasn't exactly an invalid, but flying cross-country had rendered me rather useless at the moment.

"Oh, thank you," I said. "I think I can manage getting to my room on my own. I just need to put my feet up for a minute before Babette arrives."

He nodded but proceeded to follow me down the corridor anyway.

"You flew in from Cincinnati?" he asked.

"San Francisco," I corrected.

"Ah, right. That's what I meant. Babette's told me so much about you. You knew her from beauty school."

I frowned. "College," I said. "We went to university together."

Babette had never gone to beauty school. What was he going on about?

He laughed overly loud. "Ha! I knew that. I'm just kidding. I always tell Babette she's such a beauty she must've gone to school for it." He waved his pointer fingers in the air as if making a silent drum roll.

I arrived at my hotel room door and couldn't get the key card into the slot fast enough.

Poor Charlie. He was probably just nervous to meet Babette's friends, but I felt the distinct and very real need to end our conversation.

"It was so nice meeting you." I pushed open the door to my room. "I need to make a few calls and check in at home."

He rested his hand on the doorframe and leaned in, as if waiting to be invited into my room.

What the...?

He drummed his fingers on the frame. "Did uh...did Babette mention anything to you about what time she was arriving?"

"No. I assumed you were bringing her to the event."

He laughed loudly again, showing me his overly white teeth. "Nah, I'm not allowed down there. You know, girls' night and all."

The single chair in the corner of my room beckoned me.

*How could I make him go away?*

"Oh! Listen, Charlie, I really have to put my feet up for a bit. Do you mind giving Babette this box of Ghirardelli chocolates that I brought?" Without waiting for his reply, I dug into my suitcase and produced the stunning tin of Ghirardelli premium chocolates that only a heathen could resist.

He immediately pounced on it.

"Babette loves chocolate," he said. "Only, you know, I don't let her eat it. Waistline and all," he clucked.

With that comment, I didn't feel bad about slamming the door in the man's face.

*What an absolute donkey.*

What kind of man makes a comment on his bride-to-be's waistline to her six-months-pregnant-with-twins friend!

I padded over to the hotel chair in the corner and slipped off my ballet flats. My feet instantly ballooned, and I knew it'd been a mistake. I'd never get the shoes on again. I propped my feet onto the hotel desk and grabbed my cell phone.

I missed Jim and Laurie so much it hurt.

*Why had I thought it would be a good idea to leave them?*

I dialed Jim, and he picked up on the first ring. "Hey, stranger. How's the wild bachelorette party?"

"It hasn't started yet, but I miss you guys like crazy. How's Laurie?"

"She's good. Just gave her a bottle and a bath. Here, you can talk to her." He put her on the phone, and nine-month babbling almost brought me to tears. When Jim got back on the phone, he heard the emotion in my voice. "Babe, it's only a weekend! You need this break, remember? As soon as the twins are born, there'll be no travel for a while. So enjoy yourself."

"You're right."

"How's the hotel?" he asked.

I laughed. "Honestly, this place is a dump!"

"Really?"

"Yes! I have no idea what Babette was thinking. Another thing, I just met the groom-to-be, and I don't know about him."

"What do you mean?"

"I can't put my finger on it. Just got a bad feeling from him."

"He's probably nervous," Jim reasoned. "It's hard to meet all the girlfriends at once."

I chuckled. "I guess so." I rubbed my feet and thought for a moment. "Remember I told you in college Babette always ended up with losers?"

"Kate, we aren't in college anymore. I'm sure he's a nice guy."

I sighed. "Did I ever tell you about the time she hooked up with Johnny, the pretty boy who was also a petty criminal, and he stole Babette's grandmother's heirloom sapphire bracelet that was gifted to Babette on her grandma's deathbed?"

Jim groaned. Clearly he didn't want to hear the story, but I ignored him.

"That bracelet was supposed to be *the* thing for Babette to wear at her wedding. You know, something borrowed, something blue, something old, something new."

Jim made a noise in the back of his throat that was supposed to give me the impression he was listening, but I also heard the familiar suction noise of the refrigerator opening and then the tell-tale click and fizz of what I knew for certain was a beer being opened. I'd just lost my audience, but I continued. "Babette said that bracelet could count as two things in one, because it was old and blue. She cried for weeks when pretty boy Johnny pilfered it."

"Yeah," Jim said, doing nothing to mask a big gulp of his beer.

"I don't think Babette ever recovered the bracelet. She's probably missing it now more than ever, seeing as she's about to marry."

"Uh-huh," Jim said.

"And I can't believe she's marrying this clown!"

"Give him a chance, honey."

"I will," I assured Jim as we hung up.

I glanced first at the time, then at my feet. The swelling wasn't letting up, but I'd be darned if I was going down to the party in anything less than something festive. I dug around in my suitcase and found my croc-embossed mules with the much-needed arch support. With an open heel, they fit perfectly and masked my elephant feet.

My phone pinged repeatedly, and I checked it to find a slew of photos from Jim of Laurie and our kitten, Whiskers. I pocketed the phone, armed now to rejoin the party downstairs.

Before I left the room, I crossed over to take a peek in the mirror.

The shoes complemented the outfit beautifully, giving it an extra pop of color. Go me. They were sapphire blue, which made me think of Babette's bracelet.

Was she really going to marry Charlie?

*Oh, Babette!*

# MERRY

## LESLIE LANGTRY

*I*'d seen nicer places in third-world countries. The hotel's party room looked like it was designed by an unhinged decorator who thought *despair* was a solid color scheme for a room that hosted happy events like wedding receptions.

The biggest difference between this place and the Chechen dive I frequented back in my spy days was that the furniture was largely intact, and it wasn't being run by goats. Although I must say that I did know one or two competent goats back in the day, including Baaaaart, who could make a pretty mean mai tai—as long as you didn't mind that instead of the usual umbrella with a cherry, you got a spent bullet casing on a twig.

I was still wandering around the dim, smelly room, repeatedly adjusting a fake fireplace that sagged against a wall and consulting my clipboard with the guest list without the faintest idea what I was supposed to be doing.

Why was I handling the guest list? I should've been the last person to pick. Even *I* wouldn't have picked me. I could organize a camping checklist and, back in the day, a spreadsheet of hidden nukes in Moldova. But a list of women I'd never met for a bachelorette party where I had a passing friendship with the bride-to-be?

Okay, I did know her a bit better than that. Babette and I had worked together. My name is Merry Wrath, and I'm an ex-CIA agent-turned-volunteer Girl Scout leader in my hometown of Who's There, Iowa. The reason I'm ex-CIA is because the Vice President of the United States "accidentally" outed me to get back at my senator dad. And while I didn't like leaving my chosen career, the scout gig in Iowa was growing on me, and with my precocious troop, was almost as dangerous. Anyway, for one of my very first field assignments, my cover was a pharmaceutical saleswoman. I'd found Babette through LinkedIn and asked if I could shadow her for a bit to learn the ropes.

Happily, she agreed. I spent a month following her around, learning the tricky lingo (*you* try learning to pronounce Montelukast or Xylometazoline). She wasn't like my usual friends. Babette was blonde, bubbly, and beautiful. I was decidedly more low maintenance, with a penchant for clothes I could wear to comfortably outrun a Yakuza assassin or a two-time Olympian sprinter from Bosnia who didn't take kindly to my Putin jokes.

Surprisingly, Babette and I became friends rather quickly. Babette saw what I did as acting and told me she'd always been interested in theater. We worked during the day...well, she worked and I watched her work. And we spent the evenings hanging out in bars or at her place. Turns out, she was a lot of fun.

After the month was over, I was shipped off to Syria and didn't really see her face-to-face again. Oh, we'd texted and emailed over the years, but that was it. Imagine my surprise when someone named Chelsea not only invited me to Babette's bachelorette party, but also put me in charge of invitations. By the way, never accept an invite to a Chechen bachelorette party unless you really, really like cabbage and bullets in your mai tai.

My cell went off and I looked. It was a text from Betty, the most dangerous eleven-year-old girl in Iowa and a member of my troop.

*Remember how you said we could have a sleepover at your old house?*

*No,* I texted back, *I didn't. And certainly not without adult supervision.*

*It's okay, we have Hilly. We're going to make frozen pizzas and learn about "wet work," whatever that is.*

Fantastic. The girls had Hilly Vinton with them. She was an assassin for the CIA, who wasn't an assassin, because the CIA doesn't have assassins because it's illegal (I'm required to say this due to a non-disclosure clause). Hilly loved the girls, but she thought it was okay to teach them how to hog-tie a target so he'd strangle himself if he struggled.

After texting Hilly to remind her not to turn on the oven without taking my hidden gun out first, and not to teach them anything too lethal, I consulted my clipboard for the fifth time. Why was I still holding it? I didn't know any of these people on the list. I'd already sent out the invites, so my job was done. I walked over and put it on the fake mantel of the fake fireplace, which resulted in the whole thing crashing face down on the floor. After setting it back up and handing the clipboard to the bartender, I realized I should maybe do *something*.

A few people had been in and out of the room, and I wasn't sure if I was supposed to introduce myself or just stand in a corner until Babette showed up. My best friend, Kelly, would know, and I'd ask her, but she laughed for two straight hours when I told her I was handling the invitations to a bachelorette party, so there was no way I'd give her the chance to laugh at me again by asking about proper protocol.

I did text her to say she might want to join the sleepover at my house, already in progress, and I reminded her of the gun in the oven, too. Safety first!

The people in the room must be on the guest list that I'd just handed the bartender. I'd noticed a very pregnant woman who'd set up the food table and then left. There was a gorgeous woman in sparkly shoes who seemed more like the type Babette would hang out with, and a couple of other people scattered around.

Despite the god-awful setting, someone had decorated with Dora the Explorer balloons. Yay! I was a huge Dora fan, always imagining her as a spy, with that monkey Boots as her handler. In fact, until Kelly made me buy real drapes, I was using Dora bed sheets for curtains in my living room. I decided this was a good omen, and I relaxed.

It seemed to me I should mingle. I looked down at my clothes. Maybe after I changed. A quick hop up to my room and I was back downstairs in black kitten heels and a simple, little black dress. My hair was still an unruly mess, but I'd run my hands through it and put on a little makeup so I didn't look too dowdy. It would have to do.

Upon reentering the reception room, I checked out my second-favorite thing after the bar—the food table.

I laughed out loud when I saw the *Happy Birthday Harry* cake. Obviously, the person who handled the cake and the balloons was destined to be a new friend.

"Excuse me." A woman who looked like she should've been the one to handle the invitations appeared at my elbow. She was handsomely attractive in an I'll-eat-you-for-lunch corporate way. It was obvious that she was a force to be reckoned with, and I wondered if she were related to the dominatrices who ran human resources at the CIA.

I pasted on the smile I thought went more appropriately with the moment and asked, "Can I help you?"

Like I could help anyone, unless they needed help field-stripping an AR-14 or instructions for driving through Ulaanbaatar. Helpful tip: Mongolians don't think of traffic lights as more than a three-color decoration that gives them license to race around, dodging other vehicles just before crashing. It would probably be best to hire a driver...and wear a blindfold.

The woman smiled as she looked me up and down. "Which one are you?"

She continued before I could respond. "You're obviously not the very pregnant one. And you're certainly not the New Orleans private eye. And judging by your hair, you're not the pretty stylist." The woman smiled warmly, but her eyes seemed critical. "Which makes you the one from Iowa I sent the list to."

Aha! Now I knew someone in the room by name. "You must be Chelsea. You gave me the list for the invites."

"Of course I did. You were in the CIA. That made you the best candidate for the job."

After some mental gymnastics where I totally failed to put those two things together, she continued.

"I'm the groom's sister and a friend of Babette's. I introduced them. It's so nice of you to handle the invites for me. I'm sure you found it strange since you didn't know anybody."

"Then why didn't you take care of that?" I asked bluntly. Iowan. We don't know how to be subtle.

Chelsea gave me a pitying grin as she patted me on the arm. "I got you the names from Babette's address book. The invitations you designed had an...interesting simplicity to them."

Did that mean she didn't like them? This woman seemed friendly and all, but there was an icy undertone to her words.

"You probably would've done a better job." I decided to go for flattery.

She waved her left hand dismissively. "I'm too busy for that. I'm a pharmacist, you know. From what Babette told me, you don't have a job." There was that warm smile again. "I don't mean that in a bad way. I just figured you had the time."

"Are you the one who picked this location?" I asked.

"Anyway..." Chelsea ignored my question. It was very difficult having a conversation where you were being ignored. "Take a look at the food. The cake is a scream. Babette will love it," she said in a voice that implied that *she* didn't love it. "And those balloons are so...so fun."

I spoke up in support of whoever brought them because they seemed like a kindred spirit. "I like the balloons and cake."

The woman continued to act as if I hadn't spoken. "I'm sure you all did the best you could on such short notice." She patted my arm. "Anyway, Charlie...the groom, is around here somewhere. I should introduce you to my family to make you feel more welcome." She stared into the dim recesses and pointed out a woman reading. "That's my sister."

The woman seemed to know we were talking about her and looked up in annoyance. She had thick, black-framed glasses and a hairstyle that screamed Velma from *Scooby-Doo*. An angry Velma, it appeared, as she scowled before turning back to the book. Now I knew the names of three people—Chelsea, Charlie, and their sister, Charlene—whose name I recalled from the guest list. It seemed like a win, but I kept it to myself.

"And who are the others..." I looked around, but Chelsea had left me for the bar.

What just happened? Chelsea had passive-aggressive down to an art form. She seemed nice but also seemed like a bit of a snob. Simplistic invites? What kind are you supposed to have? They were pink and had a couple of flowers on them. I thought that would be all right.

Oh well. It was only one night, and I could get along with anyone. I'd once turned a tense meeting between two, warring Chechen strongmen (whose hatred of each other stemmed from whether Persian cats or Scottish Fold cats were superior to all other breeds) into a fun karaoke night at a dive bar in Moldova that, come to think of it, must've had the same decorator as this hotel. I could do this.

Steeling myself, I took the opportunity to approach the other sister. "Hi, Charlene." I held out my hand. "I'm Merry."

"It's CHarlene," she snapped. "With a hard *Ch*! Why can't anyone remember that? It's not like it's difficult!"

"I had no idea," I apologized. "My bad."

It's been attributed to many people, but someone once said, *Diplomacy is the art of saying "nice doggy" until you can get your hands on a rock.* I was pretty sure in this case my "rock" would be a large glass of wine.

"Your invitations sucked," Charlene said. "They were way too fancy."

Maybe two large glasses of wine.

"Your sister just told me they were too simple," I said.

Charlene with a hard *Ch* sneered. "Well she's an idiot. Can you believe she got Babette the Bimbo and our brother together?"

"Babette's not a bimbo," I warned. Okay, I wasn't close enough to the bar and I didn't see any rocks, but maybe I could chuck the fake fireplace at her.

"She *never* says my name right." She got up, and I noticed she was reading *Moby Dick*. "I can't stand the woman. She has no business being in our family." And with that, she stormed away.

The party hadn't even started, and I was already screwing up. I walked over to the bar and ordered. The bartender winked and did a very dramatic pouring of the house red, fanning his green-gloved hands and using jazz fingers as if he was demonstrating that this was, in fact, a wine glass and he was, in fact, pouring wine.

"The name's Stone," he said as if introducing himself as James Bond—something spies never do, by the way. "Rock Stone."

I laughed. "You're joking."

He seemed insulted. "No. I'm not. It's my stage name."

I walked away before he could tell me anything else…or at least before I could make fun of him. As a role model for little girls, I was always trying to better myself, and mocking this guy just because he was weird kinda seemed like a bad thing.

Charlene was on the other side of the room reading as

Chelsea passed me and sidled up to Rock Stone with an empty glass. So those were Babette's future sisters-in-law? I silently wished her good luck. I had two of those...twins who were middle-aged taxidermists. Randi loved and adored me, while Ronni believed I was a pestilence on this Earth, on par with roaches, Russian figure skaters, and toxic waste.

By the way, they specialized in anthropomorphic taxidermy, where they stuffed, dressed, and posed dead animals as people doing people-y things. Often, Ronni portrayed me with a roach. Still, I cherished my mockup of a capsizing *Titanic*, complete with tiny hamsters screaming in terror. They really were talented.

I thought about what the sisters had said. Chelsea had introduced Babette to her brother, Charlie. The women must know each other professionally, what with Chelsea being a pharmacist and Babette in pharma sales. I didn't know much about Charlie, but I had met his sisters. Hopefully, he wasn't like Charlene, who seemed to loathe Babette. Perhaps Charlie was a happy medium between his sisters. I'd hate to think Babette would end up with a sister-in-law who hated her.

And to hate her over the pronunciation of her name? Was it really about that, or was Charlene one of those women you just couldn't make happy? She seemed smart. Not a lot of people read *Moby Dick* for fun—especially at a bachelorette party. Or was the book just a prop for her to hide her disgust behind?

As if she knew I was thinking of her, Charlene looked up at me, and I could swear she growled from across the room. That woman did not want to be here. Had Chelsea made her come? Had Charlie guilted her into it? As long as she didn't ruin Babette's party, I'd let her be.

I took a gulp of wine and closed my eyes. God willing, I'd gotten all of the oddball folks out of the way. Surely Babette had some nice, normal friends.

"Interesting place, isn't it?" The very pretty woman in the pink skirt and high heels was at my right elbow. "I'm Valentine."

The warmth in her voice made me relax all the way down to my shoes. Or maybe it was the wine.

I held out my hand. "I'm Merry. I remember your name from the list."

We shook hands, and I noticed her genuine smile. I was going to hang around her for the rest of the night. Hopefully, she wouldn't mind that too much.

The pregnant woman walked over to us. "Hi! I'm Kate. Are you normal? Because other than Valentine here, I haven't met anyone normal yet."

Okay. I'd found my crew for the night. Stick with them and what could go wrong?

My cell buzzed with a text from Hilly.

*Forgot and heated up oven without taking your gun out first. You're gonna need a new stove. Betty's working on plans to kidnap the mayor. She's a funny kid. Bye!*

I didn't respond and shoved my cell into my purse. It wasn't the first time I needed a new stove. I really should find another place to hide my weapon. Live and learn, right? I turned back to my new friends to find Valentine telling Kate about how she once took down a bad guy with a can of hairspray and a hat pin.

At last! Somebody normal to talk to.

# FRANKI

## TRACI ANDRIGHETTI

"*H*ere we are, lady." The cab driver eyed me in the rearview mirror. "It ain't the Ritz."

I could see that. The hotel was maybe a half a Trip Advisor star above the level of rooms by the hour. I climbed from the backseat with my charcoal overnight bag and handed the driver two twenties. "Keep the change."

"Thanks." He removed the cigar from his mouth. "Now I got a tip for you—don't spend the night in this dump." The tires squealed as he peeled out of the lot.

"And people say New Yorkers aren't friendly." I pulled up the handle of my bag and wheeled it into the lobby, which reeked of cheap cologne and pepperoni. As I approached the reception desk, a fifty-something male with thinning hair and a name tag that said *Mo* put a half-eaten Hot Pocket on the counter and wiped tomato sauce on his gray uniform.

"I'm Franki Amato. I've got a reservation for the weekend."

He eyed the computer. "I don't got anyone by that name. You sure you're in the right place?"

I'd been asking myself that very thing since the cab sped off. "Our research assistant at Private Chicks made the reservation, so it could be under my full name, Francesca Lucia Amato."

"Private Chicks?" His gaze meandered from my face to my chest. "That a men's club?"

My lips curled, and I squeezed my suitcase handle. "It's a PI firm. I'm an investigator."

He threw up his hands like he was under arrest.

"Easy, Mo. I work in New Orleans, not New York."

He resumed his search for my reservation, and I wished I'd followed my gut and declined Merry Wrath's invitation to Babette's shower. I didn't know the former, and I'd only met the latter once. But my fiancé, Bradley Hartmann, had gone to school with Babette in Boston, so he'd asked me to accept as a favor to him. The thing was that I'd already done him a favor on Babette's behalf during Mardi Gras three months earlier when he'd let her and some of her friends use his apartment while he was out of town, and the experience had verged on distasteful.

Babette had managed to get herself arrested for nudity in the French Quarter, a nearly impossible feat during Carnival season. From what the police told me, she'd topped off her Pat O'Brien's Hurricanes with a Hand Grenade at the Tropical Isle Bar, and the cocktail combo had proved explosive. While she was doing the Macarena with the Dancing Hand Grenade—the bar's green Humpty Dumpty-shaped mascot with dopey eyes, a goofy grin, and a white fuse assembly that looked like a bow—the mascot for a local chain called Dat Dog shimmied up, and he and Babette decided to swap costumes in the middle of Bourbon Street. She stripped off her Mardi Gras Queen number and was sliding into the hot dog outfit when a cop loaded her into a paddy wagon bound for New Orleans Central Lockup.

Through no fault of my own, I'd spent the night in that jail two years earlier on my thirtieth birthday. And after a large woman with a severe skin-sloughing condition had used me for a pillow, I was less than thrilled to return. But because Babette had contacted Bradley with her one phone call, he'd woken me up at three a.m. and asked me to bail her out.

When I arrived at the jail, Babette was still wearing the Dat Dog costume, and because she was naked underneath, I made her stay in it. It's a good thing I drive a convertible because the costume wouldn't allow her to sit, so I had to lay her out lengthwise across the front and backseats. The whole way to Bradley's apartment, she alternated between babbling about method acting and getting into character and singing "na na na na na na na na na na na na na na na na...DAT DOG!" like she was Batgirl in a bun. But the truth was that instead of the Batmobile, she'd turned my cute 1965 cherry-red Mustang into a wannabe Wienermobile. Frankly, the whole hot dog escapade had left a bad taste in my mouth, and I hadn't eaten one since.

Mo picked up the Hot Pocket and took a bite. "Found you. Did you want the continental breakfast?"

Based on his meal, I went with, "No."

He slid a key card envelope toward me and leaned on the counter. "Your room's on the third floor." He flashed yellow teeth flecked with mozzarella. "Want me to help you with your suitcase?"

"It's on wheels. I've got it." Given his greasy fingers and matching demeanor, I took the envelope with my fingernails and held it at arm's length. "Where's the bachelorette party for Babette Lang?"

"In the Big Apple Room. Head down the hall and take a right at the elevator."

I nodded and pulled my suitcase into the hallway. Before I pressed the elevator button, the door opened to a man and woman making out. He was leaning against the back wall, and she was all over him like the mozzarella on Mo's teeth. I couldn't say the same for her slinky silver dress, which was in serious danger of slinking off.

Fortunately, the door closed. Since I was already late, I

decided to skip the trip to my room. Given the things I'd seen in the hotel, I was confident that my black turtleneck and slacks were appropriate for the occasion, not to mention my Italian designer boots.

The event room was more Big Easy than Big Apple. Faded gold drapes, worn velvet upholstery, and filthy shag carpeting spoke of one hundred too many parties—in the 1970s. The look reminded me of a funeral parlor I'd seen outside of Baton Rouge where you could bury a loved one and buy life insurance all in one visit. And, in all honesty, the room was actually nicer than the bordello-chic furnished apartment I'd rented sight unseen from my sixty-something ex-stripper landlady.

I spotted a tape dispenser on a card table by the door and, taking a cue from Mo, made a name tag. Judging from some of the guests, I didn't want to introduce myself.

A woman in a perfectly pressed navy suit marched up. "Are you Franki, by any chance?"

"That's me." I stuck the name tag on my chest.

"I'm Chelsea, Babette's future sister-in-law. I have you on drinks, and if we're going to save this event, I need you to do better than Valentine's decorations and Kate's food."

My head retracted at her directness. "I'll do what I can, but I'm not a bartender."

"That's fine because we've already got one." She gestured to a young man with the chiseled features of a model, who was carrying a box of booze into the room. "But he's got the imagination of a rock, so he needs suggestions."

"I'm on it." I made a beeline to the bar, mostly to get away from Chelsea. I stood to one side while the bartender poured a scotch and soda for a mature woman in a curly blonde wig with red lips lined à la Lucille Ball and eyeliner that made my signature cat-eye look kittenish. Even more jarring than her exaggerated makeup were the lime-green gloves on the bartender. They went all the way up to his sizeable biceps, which explained the gloves' flower-blossom-style opening—but not entirely.

"Hey, I'm Franki." I extended my hand.

He snatched his gloved mitts away like I was holding Mo's greasy Hot Pocket. "Rock. Rock Stone."

I suppressed a smile, wondering whether Chelsea had known his name when she'd made the crack about his imagination. "Edgy, but redundant."

"Whaddaya mean?"

"You know, *rock*, *stone*, they mean the same thing?"

"Yeah." He flexed his biceps. "Hard."

*Dumb as a rock* came to mind. I wheeled my suitcase forward. "Could you stash this behind the bar?"

He scrutinized the handle.

"Careful, Rock." The painted lady swallowed a slug of scotch and pointed at my suitcase. "That handle looks cracked."

"I see that, Zelda."

*I* didn't, but I *had* squeezed it pretty hard when Mo leered at my rack. "Do you have hand injuries, or something?"

"Nah," Zelda answered for him. "He's protecting his moneymakers."

Rock carefully peeled off a glove. "Bartending's my side gig." He flexed his fingers like a proud peacock spreading its feathers. "My dream is to be a hand model."

"A *hand* model?" I repeated. "Just...*hands*?"

The woman lit a cigarette in clear view of a No Smoking sign. "That's right. I tell my clients to dream big." She exhaled at me. "I represent Rock and Babette." She squinted at my name tag. "You already got a talent agent, Frenchie?"

"*Franki*, and no. I live in New Orleans, and I'm not interested in acting."

"Too bad. With your Sophia Loren looks and height, I could make you a star—your very own baloney commercial."

"Baloney?" Rock boomed before I had time to process the processed meat offer. "You been holding out on me, Zelda?"

"Like I told you, Rock, the Oscar Mayer gig doesn't showcase all of your talents."

"Does too. I went to Higgly Piggly and saw Babette passing out wieners with her *hands*."

"Sure, and those wieners are heated. You wanna get a burn?" She blew out a mouthful of smoke to emphasize her point.

Rock retracted his hands in horror, then slipped his glove back on.

Zelda pointed her cigarette at him. "I didn't think so. Now, I didn't tell you this before because I didn't want to get your hopes up, but I'm trying to negotiate you a deal with Ball Park Franks. They sell 'em cold in the package, so there's no risk to your hands. And the best part is, you can flex your biceps when you tell customers the slogan about how they plump when you cook 'em."

Rock's eyes gleamed like the sheen on a hot dog fresh off the grill. "Heeeyyy, I see where you're going with this. I could piggy-back off the franks deal to break into bicep modeling."

I smirked. Based on Rock's IQ, the "piggyback" pun wasn't intentional.

"Slow down, Rock." Zelda stood and doused her cigarette in her highball glass. "That's a tall order even for an ace agent like me."

*So much for dreaming big.*

Zelda went to the food table, allowing me the opportunity to discuss drinks with Rock. "So what cocktails are you serving?"

"Screwdrivers and Cuba libres."

Perfect for a sad Seventies happy hour. "I think we need something more fun."

He rinsed a glass with water from the soda gun. "If you're thinking New Orleans drinks like Hurricanes and Hand Grenades, I don't know how to make them."

"Definitely not those." I didn't want a repeat of Babette during Mardi Gras, and if we were doing NOLA drinks, I'd pick The Obituary Cocktail and The Corpse Reviver #1, #2, and #3 to go with the décor. "How about limoncello martinis and Campari spritzes?"

"Are those German?"

*Mamma mia.* Apparently, *Rock* wasn't short for *Rocco.* I looked around the room for inspiration. Dora the Explorer balloons and a cake that read *Happy Birthday Harry* gave me an idea. "Let's do margaritas as our fun drink, and The Dirty Harry for those who can handle the stronger stuff."

Zelda returned to the bar with a plate of party food. She pulled out her lipstick-stained teeth, put them on a bar napkin, and gummed a cocktail wienie.

I tried not to stare at the crime scene happening in her mouth, but I couldn't help myself. I'd been a PI in NOLA for three years, and I'd never seen characters like these.

My ringtone went off. I rummaged in my hobo bag for my phone, hoping it was Bradley. This time he was going to do me a favor where Babette was concerned and get me a red-eye flight home. That cabbie was right about not staying the night.

The cell display dashed my hopes. It was my parents' number, and I promptly declined the call. The last thing I needed was for my meddling mom and Sicilian nonna to find out I was at a bachelorette party. The event was depressing enough without them calling me a *zitella*, or old maid, and whining about not having grandchildren.

As if to remind me of my old maid and childless states, a seriously pregnant woman came to the bar. She held up a picture on her phone of an infant and a cat. "How cute is this, Zelda?"

The agent was so excited she put in her teeth. "Whoa, baby! I see six-figure potential, Kate."

"Really? Oh my gosh, I can't wait to tell Jim."

"Yeah, Friskies, Purina, Fancy Feast...any one of 'em would

pounce on this deal. Just think, your cat could pay for your baby son's college at an Ivy League school."

Kate's arm dropped, and so did her eyelids. "That's my *daughter.*"

"Yowza." Rock's brow furrowed. "You sure that isn't a boy?"

"I'm her mother. I think I'd know her gender." Kate shoved her phone in my face. "Does my little Laurie look like a boy to you?"

She did, but I had to be careful because the woman was clearly hormonal. "Of course not. Look at her...pink dress."

"Right?" Kate shot a mama-bear look at the tactless talent agent and her thick-skulled client.

I pulled her aside before things got grizzly. "Between you and me, I don't think Zelda sees too well. She thought my name tag said 'Frenchie' and offered me a baloney commercial. I mean, processed meat? At the very least, I'm prosciutto di Parma."

"Oh, I so agree."

A petite woman with hair straight off the cover of *Vogue* came toward us. "You must be Franki. I'm Valentine, a friend of Babette's."

"Pleasure," I said. And it was because her heels added much needed sparkle to the room. "Speaking of the bachelorette, where is she?"

"She should be here fairly soon."

"I've got the drinks under control, so if you want I can go to the lobby and keep an eye out for her."

"That won't be necessary. We've still got time."

I let out a sigh of relief. "That's good, because I would've had to keep an eye out for Mo, the hotel clerk, too."

Valentine and Kate giggled, and I joined in. The party was looking up—until I saw a woman in a black dress and kitten heels careening toward us. She was the only other normal-looking person in the group, so I figured she was Merry, fleeing the other arriving guests, not that anyone would try to crash this party.

"Excuse me, ladies, but we've got a situation. Charlie's been hitting the booze pretty hard, and I'm not talking mai tais with cabbage and bullets. He's shooting straight tequila."

I wasn't sure where Merry got her drink recipes, but it was a good thing she'd been assigned the invitations. "Which one is Charlie?"

She unfurled her arm in the direction of a table opposite the bar. "I present to you Babette's groom-to-be."

A guy in a crumpled brown blazer and semi-unbuttoned shirt tossed back a shot and slammed the glass. He got up, stumbled to the bar, then jumped back and spun on the guests. "Who the hell brought *that* down here?"

Rock pointed a girly glove at me. "*She* did."

I stiffened. Everyone was staring except for a woman in black glasses who was reading in a corner—and Zelda who was making herself another scotch and soda. It took me a second, but I realized that Charlie was talking about my suitcase. "Uh, I was running late, so I brought my bag with me. I can run it upstairs real quick."

"What? No." Charlie scanned the guests, almost catatonic. He wiped his nose with his forearm and semi-staggered from the room.

# VALENTINE

### ARLENE MCFARLANE

"*W*hat was *that* all about?" Franki swept her sleek dark hair off her shoulders after Charlie teetered away, her gorgeous Mediterranean coloring resurfacing after briefly turning pink.

"No kidding." Kate's green eyes were as big as saucers. "You'd have thought he was trying to hide a murder the way he reacted to your suitcase."

Merry gave a shot of laughter, then sobered when she saw Kate was serious.

I was with *them*, the four of us evidently in tune to the ominous feeling in the air.

First, the groom-to-be seemed chummy with one of the guests I'd seen flitting around in a silver-sequined mini dress, and who, now that I thought about it, had disappeared from the festivities—if that's what you called this. Then, our dashing Charlie appeared bent on getting tanked, becoming rowdy, and making a scene over Franki's luggage. Was it the booze talking? Or was there something about Franki's suitcase we didn't know?

This party was dying before it even began. If Babette didn't show up soon, everyone would abandon ship, and the four of us would have to eat the birthday cake alone—which wouldn't be all bad since it was chocolate with hazelnut mousse inside. Maybe we could call Harry and invite him for a slice.

Suddenly, someone near the window cried, "She's coming!"

Hallelujah!

I turned to Franki in her stunning Italian boots. "Hit the lights?"

She gave me a thumbs-up, her romantic, cat-shaped eyes gleaming. "I'm on it."

"Okay, everyone." I raised my hand, displaying more confidence than I felt. I didn't wish to step on any toes, but I wanted Babette to have the time of her life, and this cheer of support would be a good start. "You know what to say when she walks through the door."

"What?" the dowdy bookworm with helmet hair and thick glasses snarled like she was Little Jack Horner stuck in his corner.

Merry leaned in. "That's Charlene, with a hard *Ch*. Isn't she pleasant?"

I grinned at Merry. "She's been glaring at me all night. I'm thinking of offering to take my lipstick and spread a smile on her face." Hey, if I could turn one of my clients' daughters into a goddess despite her aversion to chemical smells and dislike for makeup, I could do wonders for Charlene, even with a hard *Ch*.

Merry barked out a laugh. "She could use the makeover."

For Charlene's sake, I explained. "On three, two, one, we'll cry *Surprise!*"

Kate clapped her swollen hands, her eyes full of excitement. "I can't wait to see Babette. It's been too long." She snickered, rubbing her tummy. "More than a baby ago."

Seemed we all knew Babette from different stages, but we were in this together until the bitter end. Judging from how the night was unfolding, that might be sooner than later.

Attempting to remain positive, I wrapped my arm around

Kate's shoulder and gave her a squeeze. The day hadn't exactly been a ten on the Valentine scale of cheer and glitter, so thank goodness I had the warmth of these new *normal* friends. They were turning out to be the best part of my weekend.

Everyone hushed, the lights went down, and we heard a high-heeled *click-clack click-clack* come down the hall. Yep. Babette had undoubtedly changed from her hot dog costume into one of her sexy outfits that accentuated her abundant hour-glass figure.

"Three, two, one," Merry counted, and the lights went up.

"Surprise!"

The word died on everyone's lips, the surprise on us.

The woman who entered the room was tall, blonde, and voluptuous, a replica of Babette, but she was *not* our bachelorette.

"*Candace Needlemeyer!*" I didn't need a mirror to see the steam piping out my ears.

"Candace?" Merry, Kate, and Franki—who'd returned to the group—asked in unison, swiveling their heads from my shocked face to the phony in red stilettos standing in the doorway.

I rolled my eyes so far to the back of my head I saw the tiny, wigged lady at the bar pick her teeth up off the floor. Ha! Someone else shocked at Medusa's arrival.

I lowered my voice and got a grip, centering on my three friends. "Candace owns a beauty salon three blocks from mine. She's the thorn in my side, the pain in my butt, the bane of my existence." Okay, I failed miserably at getting a grip.

Kate gave a hesitant grin. "I take it she's not your BFF."

I choked at the thought. "Not only is she *not* my best friend forever, but she spends more time trying to steal business than I can count. I hate lowering myself, speaking this way about another person, but Candace makes the Wicked Witch of the West look like Mother Teresa."

Franki angled a side-eye at me. "She's dressed like a regular on Bourbon Street, which is perfect for this party."

Merry looked over at her clipboard that was sitting on the bar. "I don't recall sending her an invite."

"Of course you didn't send her an invite. Does the Wicked Witch of the West even have an address?" I balled my hands into fists and took a heavy breath. "There's something fishy going on, and I aim to find out what it is. Excuse me while I ask Candace what end of the hotel she parked her broom."

Speaking of which, why in heaven's name were we hosting a bachelorette party for Babette in a hotel that had patches of shag carpet, faded drapes, and a fake fireplace that couldn't remain upright? Was this someone's idea of a joke?

I glanced at Charlie's sister Chelsea in her uptight blue suit—something you'd never see me in unless it had a flattering neckline and some sparkle. For that matter, I could make any outfit work, given the right hairstyle and accessories. But our soon-to-be sister-in-law seemed the type to be particular about more than her crisp wardrobe.

So why this place? Had she picked it to be vindictive? Had something happened between her and Babette? Babette had told me she'd met Charlie through Chelsea, so why had the woman chosen this rundown hotel to celebrate this special night?

I decided to give Chelsea some slack. Maybe she had reserved a nice place, and the deal fell through at the last minute, leaving her few choices on another suitable venue.

I swung my head back to Candace, more pertinent things at the forefront. I slung my bag over my back since I hadn't found a safe place to put it in this joint, and, suppressing the knot in my stomach, marched over to the troublemaker.

I stopped a foot in front of Candace and decided to put my best face forward. I wouldn't get anywhere by being nasty. I looked up into her baby blues and offered a civil greeting.

"*Valentine.* What are *you* doing here?" She looked down her nose at me in my cute dress and chic heels. "Seems everywhere I go, little Miss Beaumont shows up."

*Just keep smiling.* "I'm here because I was invited to Babette's party. You?"

She fluffed her shoulder-length blonde hair, then yanked up her signature red tube top before her fake boobs fell out. "I'm here for the party, too."

I scanned the hall, sure that Candace had made a wrong turn somewhere. "This is a bachelorette party, not a brothel-ette party."

"Hardy-har-har." Not denying she was a trollop, she took a sweep of the room, then aimed a red-dagger nail at me, her collagen-filled lips plumped to nearly bursting. "I didn't need an invite to the party. Babette and I go way back."

"Back to where?" It was an innocent question.

She blew air out her nose, apparently riled by my cheekiness. "For your information, Valentine, Babette and I went to Drama Club together when we were adolescents."

"*You?* Went to Drama Club?" This was too comical, even for my ears.

"Yes," she boasted. "Babette and I performed in several local plays."

"Like what? *Death of a Salesman?*" I couldn't help myself.

She squinted meanly at me. "Plays by Gilbert and Sullivan. Tennessee Williams. Shakespeare. The last play we did together was *Taming of the Shrew.*"

"Let me guess. You were the shrew."

She crossed her arms in front. "Always with the jokes, aren't you, Valentine?"

I felt the corners of my lips slide up.

"Never mind that." She tapped her red stiletto on the floor, two inches in front of a chunk of shag carpet—probably what her whole house was scattered with—and looked pointedly around the room. "What have you done with Babette?"

Like I'd stuffed her in a closet or something. "Babette hasn't arrived yet. But when she does, I'm sure she'll tell you to fire up your broom and take off."

"I don't think so. Babette's mom told my mom about the party. She'll be happy to see me."

Oy. I might've been stuck with Candace being here, but I didn't need to further the conversation. I peered over my shoulder at Little Jack Horner, then back at her. "Why don't you grab a plate of food and sit in the corner with that woman reading. I'm sure she could use a friend."

Candace nosed over my shoulder. "Maybe I will. What's her name?"

"Charlene." Just to be unhelpful, I neglected mentioning the hard *Ch*.

Candace bustled by me without so much as a *thank you*, leaving in her wake a small, bald man dressed in clothes a shade too big, scrutinizing the place like he had a bone to pick.

*Now what?*

"May I help you with something?" Despite being in heels, it wasn't often I had to look down at someone when speaking.

"No, no." He frowned, his whine grating on the ears. "I'm merely wondering if she'th here." He bobbed his shiny head past my shoulder in an earnest search.

I overlooked his slight lisp and followed his gaze. "She?"

"*Babette*." His frown deepened. Clearly annoyed I needed to ask.

"And you are?"

"Thtanley, her boss at Higgly Piggly."

Of course. The tightwad. I clenched my shoulder strap to my side in case he saw the teeny mustards Babette had thrown in my bag.

"She thaid she had a party to attend here," he went on, "but I told her there'th no party until she hands out thothe thamplers at the Falls."

My eyebrows arched into my hairline, my heart giving a pang

for Babette, employed by this turkey. "You made her work...after work?"

He squinted at me, his lisp more pronounced in anger. "Lithen. I have a lot of money invethted in thothe wieners. You think it'th eathy getting a deal to parade our goodth at the Falls? Every frankfurter company in the country would die for that gig."

"Then why didn't *you* dress as the wiener?" Oops, did I say that out loud?

He stood on his tiptoes and shook his stubby finger in my face. "If Babette wanth to keep her job, she needth to walk that thtrip until every latht thauthage is gone." He relaxed and checked his watch strapped to his wrist. "Who knowth? With any luck, she may be here before Chrithmath."

Could you believe this guy? No wonder Babette hadn't contacted me. *Handing out wieners at the Falls.* Now I'd heard everything. "Let me get this straight. You came here, making sure Babette *wasn't* here."

He rocked back on his tiny feet, a cheesy smile in place. "Now we're talking the thame language."

The only language I wanted to talk with this guy was one made of hand gestures...in Italian. I spied Franki with the others. I bet *she'd* "talk" with Stanley until his face turned the color of Candace's shoes.

I clutched his wrist and looked at the time. "Babette's only ten minutes late. I'm sure she'll be here soon."

He jerked his arm away from me. "Yeah. Probably." His whiny tone was getting under my skin. "Until then, I thee my pal, Rock, behind the bar."

Rock? A pal? Where was the connection there?

He gave an irritating chuckle. "Maybe I'll grab a drink while we wait for Babette."

*Sure, why not? Since this now seemed to be an open event.* I poked my head out the door. *Anyone else want to join the party?*

Stanley straightened his shoulders, trotted to the bar, and climbed onto a stool next to the tiny woman with the matted wig. Truthfully, they made a nice pair.

I thought about Stanley's words, then rolled back to Babette's unreadable mood earlier. I could understand she wasn't thrilled with her job, but I knew Babette. Wieners or no wieners, she would've contacted me or one of the others tonight if she were running late. No. Something must've happened, and the more time that passed, the more my imagination was running away with me.

Maybe I was overanalyzing things, but I didn't like the unease climbing my spine. The last time I felt this way, a dead body crashed to my feet from a tall tidal wave above.

I looked up. No chance of anything crashing to my feet in here except maybe a few ceiling tiles.

For my own peace of mind, I dug out my phone and tried Babette's cell.

No answer. Of course. Babette was handing out wienies at the Falls. Or *had* she met trouble? She was good at that, but what kind of trouble could she have met?

I was pondering this when I spotted Candace with a plate of food park herself beside the bookworm, disrupting her from her reading. A tense moment went by, then, above the din, I heard, "That's Charlene with a hard *Ch!*"

# KATE

## DIANA ORGAIN

 o Do:

1. ~~Figure out food for Babette's bachelorette party.~~
2. ~~Call home.~~
3. See Niagara Falls.
4. Try not to miss Laurie and Jim too much.
5. Does this hotel have a spa?
6. Where is Babette?

I GLANCED AT MY WATCH. Babette was now officially one hour late. Not the end of the world, but still, everyone was getting impatient and drunk. Not me, of course, which was part of the problem. My bladder could barely hold half a cup of soda water before I was off to the restroom.

Next to me at the bar on my right was Babette's rotten boss from the grocery store, whose name I learned was Stanley, yammering with the bartender and the talent agent who'd insulted Laurie. On my left, the barstools that had recently accommodated my new best friends were vacant. Valentine, Franki, and Merry were at the food table, which I was religiously avoiding because all I wanted to do was eat cake, and honestly, if I indulged any more, even my maternity pants wouldn't fit.

Suddenly a hush came over the room, and I bolted upright ready to shout *Surprise!* to Babette, but when I turned I also was silenced.

A blonde in a slinky sequined mini dress sauntered into the room and stalked over to the empty stool next to me. She clutched something under her arm and flashed me a toothy grin as she sat beside me.

"Vodka martini, dirty," she said to the bartender.

The bartender pulled a face and tore himself away from Stanley and Zelda.

"Screwdrivers and Cuba libres are the signature cocktails—"

"Too much sugar in a screwdriver with that orange juice," she said. "Have to watch my sugar." Vodka martini woman in the second skin dress swiveled on her barstool and placed the package she'd carried into the room onto the bar.

I frowned.

The package was not a gift for Babette as I'd assumed, or rather it was, but...it was a gift from me. Dirty-martini woman ripped into the box of Ghirardelli chocolates I'd brought for Babette. She unwrapped a foil-covered chocolate cable car and shoved it into her mouth with a laugh.

"Chocolate?" she offered.

"No," I said, biting my tongue.

*How had this blonde bimbo ended up with the box of chocolates I'd intended for Babette?*

Could Charlie have been so crass as to give it to the woman instead of my friend?

"I'm Amber," she volunteered.

"Kate," I said.

Amber licked her lips. "Man! These are unreal!" She flipped

over the box and studied the label. "Premier chocolate. I imagine once you have these, you're just ruined for plain chocolate. Or heck, plain M&M's." She giggled to herself and popped a mini brown replica of the Golden Gate Bridge into her mouth.

It could be a different box of chocolates...

*What were the chances it was the same box I bought for Babette?*

I glanced around the room. Was there someone else here from San Francisco? Not likely. San Francisco wasn't a great airport hub to the East Coast either, so the idea of someone buying the box in an airport shop was ludicrous.

"How do you know Babette?" I asked Miss Size-Zero-Pounding-Chocolate-Like-It-Was-Going-Out-Of-Style.

*So much for watching her sugar intake!*

"I don't," she said with her mouth full. She licked chocolate off her teeth. "I'm a friend of Charli...Charlene and Chelsea."

Rock snorted as he put the martini glass in front of her and refilled my club soda.

She quirked an eyebrow at him. "You know it's true. Charlene and Chelsea love me."

"I don't think you were exactly invited—"

"I was so," she said, interrupting Rock. She squared her shoulders. "Chelsea has made everything very clear to me." She over enunciated the word *everything*, then proceeded to slurp the martini.

Rock shrugged and returned to chat with the talent agent, who for her part turned and meowed at me.

Goodness, what kind of quack den had I stumbled upon?

"Don't wander off too far, Rock," Amber warned. "I'm going to need a second, pronto." She stuffed another chocolate shaped like Coit Tower into her mouth, then said to me, "I'm going to eat this whole box. I deserve it."

At the mention of chocolate, the twins did a somersault and rebounded off my bladder. They were demanding that either I eat a piece of chocolate immediately or rush to the restroom. I decided on the latter and stood, but Amber grabbed my arm.

"Where are you off to?"

"Excuse me, I need to use the restroom."

"Hang on." She stuffed the final piece into her mouth and hopped off the barstool. "I'll go with you." She slammed a hand onto the bar. "Barkeep! One for the road!"

Rock rolled his eyes, then proceeded to mix her cocktail.

I looked around the room. Seriously, where was Babette?

Leaning over the bar, I called out to Stanley. "Have you heard from Babette? Do you think she's on her way yet?"

He shrugged, looking completely disinterested in anything besides his rum and coke. "No, but if she knowth what'th good for her, she'll hand out thothe wieners before she gets here. She should be here thoon."

*That's a relief.*

Rock served Amber her second vodka martini, which she promptly drained. She plunked the chocolates onto the barstool as a way of saving her seat, then hooked her arm through mine, and staggered awkwardly in her heels.

"You're so cute with your pregnant belly," she said. "I hope to be a mom one day. Your first?"

"No. I have a nine-month-old at home," I said.

Amber's eyes widened and she worked her mouth. It appeared the math was too much for her.

"Oh…" she said. "Let's pee!"

Although not the most elegant words in the English language, I was certainly happy she'd uttered them.

We walked past the food table, and when Amber spotted the Dora balloons she spontaneously combusted into tears.

*Oh, dear!*

What in the world?

And I thought I was the hormonal one.

I'd forgotten how being the only sober person at a party can be a real downer.

Amber clutched at my arm, black streaks of mascara rushing down her face.

"Is everything all right?" I asked.

From the food table, Valentine and Franki caught my eye, both horrified at the spectacle Amber was creating.

"Where's Babette?" I mouthed to Valentine.

Valentine grimaced and shrugged.

My investigator instincts fired. How could Babette be so late to her own party? I know her boss made her work late, but still, she should've been here by now.

Worry twisted in my gut...at least it felt like worry and not the twins.

I ushered Amber past the fake fireplace and exited the room into the corridor. The restrooms were at the end of the hallway near the elevator.

"I drank those martinis too quickly," Amber said.

*You think?*

"The ladies' room is right here," I said, maneuvering her down the hallway.

Just as I pushed open the door boasting a wooden carving of a pink stiletto, the men's restroom door swung open and Charlie emerged.

I was ready to ask him about the box of chocolates he was supposed to give to Babette, but my question got derailed.

"Amber?" he slurred.

Amber stiffened on my arm, then turned to Charlie. "Hey, what's up?"

"What...what are you doing here?" Charlie stuttered.

"You don't remember?" Amber shrieked.

Charlie rubbed at his eyes. "I...no...I..."

Oh no. By the looks on their faces and the tension in the air, I was about to be caught in the middle of an argument, and I really needed to use the restroom!

I attempted to loosen Amber's grip on my arm and make a break for the ladies' room, but she gripped me harder. "Can you believe this guy?"

"Amber…" Charlie said. "Please—"

"Get lost! You loser!" Amber marched into the ladies' room, yanking me along with her.

The restroom was surprisingly clean and comfortably furnished. There was a large velvet lemon-colored settee that Amber promptly threw herself on facedown.

"I hate him," she wailed, streaking the butter settee with mascara.

"Why? What's he done to you?" I raced to the sink and grabbed a hand towel.

When I went to hand it to Amber, she swatted it away, a look of pure disgust on her face. My purse vibrated, and I recognized it as my cell phone.

I tossed the towel to Amber and dug into my purse, hoping it was a call from Babette. Instead, I recognized Jim's cell number. My heart lurched.

*Please God, let everything be all right with Laurie!*

"Hello? Is everything okay?" I asked Jim, my voice cracking.

"Oh, hi, honey. Yeah, no worries. I pocket dialed you. Are you okay? You sound off."

Amber shot me a morose look. "Who's that?" She added in a sing-song mocking voice, "Babette?"

"It's my husband," I said to her.

She wiped her nose on the hand towel. "Of course, you have a loving, caring husband. Everyone does. Everyone but me," she howled, reeled back on the settee, and almost slipped off.

I reached out for her and practically toppled myself. Geez, my balance being pregnant with the twins had been lacking from the beginning and was only getting worse.

"Jim, I'm going to have to call you back."

"Is that Babette crying?" he asked, alarmed. "Is the wedding off?"

"No, no. The wedding's not off."

Amber wrenched herself forward. "The wedding's off?"

I held up a finger to her. "No. No. Just give me a minute."

She slumped onto the settee again and truthfully looked a little green around the gills.

I covered the mouthpiece of my cell phone. "You okay?" I asked Amber.

She waved me away.

I slid into one of the stalls and asked Jim, "So everything's all right at home?"

"Yeah. I just put Laurie down. She sacked out."

I smiled. "Thank you for sending me the pictures of Laurie and Whiskers. I think I landed Whiskers a commercial deal."

Jim chuckled. "Oh yeah? She's a looker."

We giggled together, and I heard Amber groan.

"I gotta go, honey," I said. "Talk to you later, 'k?"

"Sure thing," he said, and hung up.

I heard Amber shuffle from the settee to the stall next to me. She closed the door hard, rattling my stall door as she locked hers. I relieved myself quickly and exited to the sink, waiting for any telltale sounds from her stall to indicate that she hadn't passed out.

I washed my hands and dried them. Then waited.

My phone pinged, and I checked to see that Jim had sent me a sleeping picture of Laurie and, next to her, Whiskers asleep with a paw over her own eyes. Too cute for words.

I studied the picture.

Laurie decidedly did not look like a boy. With those cute strawberry blonde curls framing her tiny face. And the pink sleeper? *Please.* She was a perfect, cherubic feminine doll.

And she was mine.

I was suddenly glad that Zelda didn't think Laurie was child-model material. Who wanted that for their baby, anyway? Everyone knew what happened to child stars. Drug addictions, prison, suicides. Every unimaginable tragic end one could think of.

Whiskers on the other hand...

Whiskers had a money-shot look.

She photobombed every picture. She loved the camera.

*Purina, was it?*

Amber sniffled behind the closed door of the stall, and I was reminded what I was doing in the ladies' room.

"Hey, Amber. You okay?"

"Mmm," she muttered. "Yeah, go on ahead."

"I can wait for you."

"Mmm-mmm. No. You should go see if Babette's here." She emphasized Babette's name again in that nasal sing-song way. "I'll be out in a minute."

"Okay, see you later," I said, pushing open the bathroom door.

After all, I was pregnant with twins. I'd probably be back in the ladies' room before Amber was ready to emerge, anyway.

As the door closed behind me, I heard Amber wail Babette's name again.

Boy, she really did have it out for Babette.

I wondered why.

*And what did Charlie have to do with it all?*

*Did he give Amber my chocolates?*

# MERRY

## LESLIE LANGTRY

*ypothetically*, the text read from Hilly, *how much do you like your garage? On a scale of 1 to 13? 13 being the most, obviously.*

*130,000*, I texted back. *Do not mess with my garage.* I hesitated. *What were you thinking of doing?*

*It's totally hypothetical*, Hilly texted. *Asking for a friend.*

I responded with a question to which I already knew the answer. *Would this friend be an eleven-year-old precocious girl named Betty?*

There was an emoji that looked like an eye roll. *No, because it's hypothetical, so it's a hypothetical friend. Duh.*

*Don't do anything to my garage*, I warned again.

*Another hypothetical question*, Hilly texted. *How long do you think it takes to rebuild a garage before the person who owns it comes back from a weekend trip? And follow-up question. Do you have a hammer?*

This time I texted my husband and suggested he walk over to my old house and take a fire extinguisher, just in case. When we got married, Rex and I lived across the street from each other. His house was nicer, bigger, with better furniture, and, I'll be completely honest—cleaner—so we both lived there. Because I didn't want to part with my little ranch house, I kept it as a base of operations for troop meetings, overnight guests, and so on. Right about now, I was regretting that.

What a strange evening this was turning out to be. And I'd been to Kim Jong-un's thirtieth birthday party. The diminutive dictator was dressed like the Greek god Apollo (although why he was wearing assless chaps was anyone's guess), and arrived in a gold chariot pulled by ten sickly-looking Komodo dragons (and pushed by twenty starving North Koreans). There was a knockoff of the Mormon Tabernacle Choir singing dirty sea shanties about Kim's alleged gigantic manhood, and the theme was—Dress as your favorite dictator who, of course, is less powerful than our Dear Leader.

I went as Catherine de Medici, not realizing that the ruler had to be from recent history. There were twenty-two of Madam Mao, fifty of Imelda Marcos, and one very confused-looking Angela Merkel (who actually won first prize, which was a date with Dear Leader). I later found out that she was the *real* Angela Merkel, whose driver had misunderstood the directions to a K-Pop concert in Seoul.

Franki sidled up to me and asked, "Who's the drunk Kate helped to the bathroom?" I'd noticed that the New Orleans private eye was aware of everything going on around us. It was good to have her around, even if we didn't expect anything untoward to happen.

"I'm not sure." My clipboard might have the answers, but it was all the way across the room, which seemed really far. Besides, my duties were done. It was time to relax and hang out with my new friends while we waited for Babette.

"I heard her name's Amber." Valentine smoothed a stray strand of her unbelievably gorgeous hair. "It's nice of Kate to help her to the bathroom."

I nodded. "It looks like she needs a moment to pull herself together. Did you guys see her gobbling those chocolates? Who brings candy for themselves to a party?" I wasn't sure if I was saying that out of respect for decorum or jealousy because she didn't share with me. Hopefully, my new friends would think it was out of respect.

"She doesn't seem like someone Babette would want here," Valentine said, her hands in fists at her side as she glared at the other obnoxious woman who'd just arrived.

Oh, right. That Candace woman who barged in appeared to be Valentine's evil, slutty nemesis. Well, a slutty enemy of my friend becomes *my* slutty enemy, or something like that. I made a mental note to keep an eye on her.

"Anyone know where Babette is?" Franki looked around.

"Oh!" Valentine said with a start. "I forgot to tell you. Stanley, her boss, is here." She gave a curt head tilt to the bald man taking up space at the bar. "He said she has to hand out samples at the Falls. That's why she's late. He's checking up on her to make sure she didn't skip out to come here."

"He's making her miss her own party? I don't like him." I wiggled my eyebrows suggestively. "Want me to take him out back and teach him how to be nice to his employees?"

Franki smiled. "Nah. Then you'd end up in jail, and we'd miss the party bailing you out."

Awww, that was nice! We were already at bailing-me-out-of-jail friend status!

I shook my head. "I'd be willing to bet the city jail is nicer than this place."

Franki pursed her lips. "On second thought, maybe you should take Stanley out back. I wouldn't mind missing this shindig to bail you out."

There was a shout, and we all turned to see Chelsea making a beeline for us. Charlene glowered at her sister's back before diving back into *Moby Dick*. With all the weirdness going on around us, I had to wonder if her choice of book was turning into a metaphor. But who was the white whale? I hoped it wasn't me.

"Where's Babette?" Chelsea pointed at the door. "Why's Amber here? And who is that bimbo in the stilettos?"

Valentine repeated the story of Babette's boss being here to check up on her.

Chelsea's scowl deepened. "Screw that! Babette should be here by now! And the bimbo?"

Valentine grimaced. "I know her from back home. Apparently, she and Babette were in a Drama Club together when they were kids."

"She wasn't on the list," I added helpfully. "Neither was anyone named Amber."

Chelsea narrowed her eyes as if she were aiming lasers at me. "You're in charge of the guest list. Throw her out!"

I held up my drink, even though it was sadly empty. "No thanks. My work shift is over, and my fun shift has just begun."

Chelsea turned an alarming shade of red as if she were sunburned by her own fury. "You could at least pour Amber into a taxi and send her home. She has no business being here!"

"And why is that?" Franki asked.

"Because she's Charlie's ex, that's why!" Chelsea actually stamped her foot like a toddler. "She's probably here to get him back!"

"Well," I said slowly, "how are we supposed to know something like that? It seems again like the guest list should've been your job."

"Argh!" The woman threw her hands in the air and stomped out of the room, presumably to find Amber and toss her out.

"That was fun," I mumbled.

Valentine looked pensive. "Do you think she's right...that Amber crashed the party to win Charlie back?"

Franki nodded. "Looks that way. They're both acting weird—which implies that maybe Charlie doesn't want to get married?"

"This should be entertaining." And we had front row seats to the mayhem. "We're going to need another drink. I'll buy a round. What'll you guys have?"

MINUTES LATER, I found myself discussing the finer points of existential philosophy with Rock Stone, bartender/hand model. Okay, I wasn't. I was arguing with him about drinks. Any guy who picked the stage name Rock Stone didn't have any brain cells to spare for any philosophy more complicated than something you'd see on Sesame Street.

"I just want another glass of wine. Why is that so hard?" I toyed with threatening to break a finger, but he might faint at the thought of it. Of course, then I could pour my own drinks. The idea had merit.

Rock looked around the bar. "I'm supposed to push the signature cocktails. Chelsea wants us to because we over-ordered the stuff for those particular drinks."

"But you have wine right there," I pointed out.

"Fine." He glanced around nervously. "What do you want? Yellow or…" Rock frowned at the array before him. "Reddish?"

"You mean white," I corrected before I realized I'd just made things worse by doing so.

Rock lifted a bottle of chardonnay out of the cooler as if he were pulling a tube of plutonium out of a cold-storage cooler. He then waved one hand over it like a magician—perhaps in hopes that it would turn it into a desperate Hollywood producer in dire need of a hand model for a movie.

"It really looks yellow. Why would you call it white?" He scowled as he displayed it dramatically to me across the palms of his hands, fingers wiggling.

"Fine." I gave up. "Just give me that."

I looked over and gave the girls a thumbs-up, noticing that

Kate was back with the crew. And she wasn't the only one. Amber staggered over to the bar, her melted mascara indicating she'd been crying and giving her the strange appearance of a member of the Insane Clown Posse. She pulled out the barstool and picked up the box of chocolates next to me I'd evidently missed. Finally managing to balance herself on the stool, she proceeded to eat the chocolates.

Hey! I recognized those! Ghirardelli! Chocolate was kind of my favorite food group, and this San Francisco confectioner was one of the best. Wait...San Francisco? My *spy*-dy senses began tingling.

I looked over at Kate. She was from San Francisco, right? And she was glaring daggers at Amber as she guzzled the chocolates. Did Kate bring those for Babette? And if so, why in the hell was Amber eating them?

*Yeesh, Merry! You're not investigating anything,* I chastised myself. If Kate did bring those for our missing party girl and wasn't chewing Amber out for eating them, I should just stay out of it. Unless Kate wanted me to waterboard her in the alley— which had the added bonus of placating Chelsea.

Besides, it wasn't like there was a body or anything. We were all here to celebrate Babette. I needed to let it go.

Amber sort of fell off the stool and wobbled precariously. "I don't feel so good."

For some reason, she stepped around the bar, next to Rock, who looked like he'd rather use a cheese grater on his precious hands than let the woman near him.

"Oooh..." Amber wobbled again.

"Are you all right?" I asked, mostly because that was what a responsible adult would do.

Amber's eyes grew wide as she stared at me. For one brief moment, she stood utterly still.

"Nope," she said finally as her eyes rolled upwards and she fell backwards, crashing to the floor.

I ran around the bar and stared at Rock, Amber sprawled out between us.

"Why didn't you catch her?" I demanded as I knelt beside the woman.

Rock shrugged. "I didn't want to damage my hands." He pulled off his gloves, and I thought I heard him murmur, *Are you all right, girls?*

I checked Amber for a pulse, but she didn't have one. Now there was a body. I took out my cell to call for an ambulance and noticed Rex had texted me.

*Why do you have a flamethrower...and how do you feel about having a carport instead of a garage?*

I did not text him back.

"What am I supposed to do now?" Rock whined. "She's lying behind the bar! I can't work like this!"

"She's dead," I snapped. "I think that's a higher priority right now."

Rock threw up his arms. "Well, that's just great. There go my tips! I was saving up for a pair of Super Shield cotton protective gloves, too!"

I stared at him for a second before pointing to his right hand. "Is that a hangnail?"

He screamed like a little girl and shoved on his gloves.

I called 9-1-1.

# FRANKI

## TRACI ANDRIGHETTI

*M*erry hovered over me while I attempted chest compressions on Amber. "Hang in there, Franki. The ambulance is coming."

I was trying, but Amber's chest was as hard as Rock's biceps. Cadavers were called stiffs for a reason, but rigor mortis didn't set in this fast. "Honestly, it's too late for the paramedics."

"This party is starting to feel like my Havana assignment when Fidel Castro up and died."

If I hadn't been preoccupied with saving a life, I would've asked her to elaborate. Cuba seemed like an odd place for a Girl Scout troop leader unless the girls were trying to earn their Banned Travel Badge.

Merry crouched beside me. "So, what do you think? Alcohol poisoning?"

Reluctantly, I stopped pumping and sat on my heels. A couple of years before, I'd investigated the death of another Amber, a dancer found in a bathtub on a strip club stage with a bottle of Amaretto. But the booze hadn't killed her, and I didn't believe it had killed this Amber either.

"She's got the symptoms of alcohol poisoning." I pointed to

her face. "Enlarged pupils, blue lips and fingernails, foam at the mouth. But something caused her chest muscles to seize up, which makes me think she's got another toxin in her system."

Someone gasped behind me, and I turned to see Kate with a look as fierce as a mama bear's. She thrust her arm at Zelda. "She did it."

Zelda swallowed a cocktail wienie and put in her teeth. "*Me!* You're the one who led her out of the party. What'd you do? Slip her a mickey?"

Kate recoiled. "She was upset, so I took her to the ladies' room."

Valentine stared down at the dead body and took a steadying breath. Then she put her arm around our pregnant friend. "Kate was just trying to keep the mood festive."

*Keep it festive? This party was dead on arrival.* I glanced at Amber and issued a silent apology for my choice of expression.

Zelda climbed off her barstool and hobbled over to me. "You don't gotta be Columbo to know the timing of her little bathroom visit is suspicious."

"I'm pregnant," Kate growled in keeping with mama-bear mode. "I'm in there every fifteen minutes."

"Don't listen to her, Frenchie. She's got a hot temper, and she's vindictive."

"It's *Franki*," I ground out in a tone not unlike Kate's.

Zelda straightened her wig. "She's got it in for me because I don't want to represent that baby boy of hers."

Kate clenched her fists and stomped her foot. "Laurie is a *girl*."

Valentine patted her shoulder. "And when her hair grows longer, it's going to be fabulous."

Mo slithered in from the lobby. His uneasy gaze traveled from Merry to me. "Hey, uh, can you guys take it down a notch? I'm trying to watch *Weekend at Bernie's*."

The reference to a movie about a corpse partying at his own party was a real party pooper. The way the bachelorette bash was deteriorating, I wouldn't have been surprised if it turned into *Weekend at Babette's*. "In case you hadn't noticed, Mo, a guest has passed, and we're waiting on an ambulance."

He looked down at Amber and ran his greasy Hot-Pocket hands up and down his shirt. "So, uh…" He leaned in. "Will there be any cops?"

My patience flatlined. "A young woman has died. What do you think?"

"Gotcha." He puffed out his cheeks and looked to the side. Then he took a couple of steps backwards, turned, and shot through the door.

Merry took off after him. "I'm on it!"

She seemed like she could take the guy, so I didn't offer to help. After all, she had experience rounding up wayward Girl Scouts.

I turned to Kate. "When you took Amber to the bathroom, did she say why she was upset?"

"Not really, but we ran into Charlie in the hallway, and she was furious with him. He seemed pretty shaken by it."

Chelsea stormed from a table where she'd been huddled with other guests. "My brother was shaken because Amber crashed his fiancée's celebration."

"I'd like to hear that from him, if you don't mind." I looked around the room. "Where is he, by the way?"

She blanched. "He probably went for help. I'll find him."

"You do that," I called after her. "He's a prime suspect."

Valentine blinked her long lashes once from Chelsea to me like she was considering something. "Your PI training telling you something is off about Charlie?"

"That, and every other episode of *Dateline NBC*, *48 Hours*, and *20/20* says the significant other is usually the main culprit." I looked at Amber's lifeless body, and her silver-sequined mini dress sparked a memory. *She was the woman I saw making out with someone in the elevator. But who was she kissing?*

Surely it wasn't Mo from the front desk. The guy ate pepperoni Hot Pockets, and not even a drunk, despondent woman would lock lips with that.

Charlie was a more likely makeout suspect, since he was her ex. But I couldn't rule out any of the men at the party, except for maybe bald, sixty-something Stanley, sitting at the bar. A more pressing question was what Amber had been eating and drinking before she died. If poison was a factor, everyone at the party could be at risk.

I raised my arms. "Attention, please. For your safety, the food and drink are now off limits."

Groans erupted.

A box of chocolates on the bar caught my eye. I didn't remember seeing them on the food table. "Where'd the Ghirardelli come from?"

Kate slid onto a barstool. "I think they're the ones I brought from San Francisco for Babette."

"You *think?*"

She slipped off a shoe to massage a swollen foot. "I asked Charlie to give them to her, but then Amber turned up with the box." Kate's lips thinned, and she snorted. "He didn't want Babette to have the chocolates because he said he was watching her weight."

My cat-eyelined eyes went lioness. *Another reason to suspect him.* "When was this?"

"Right after I got here, when I went up to my room to—"

"Hang on. You were in your hotel room with Babette's fiancé?"

She blinked. "I didn't let him in. What do you think I am? A cheap floozy?"

I eyed her baby bump. "I mean, not in your present condition."

"Ooh!" She shoved on her shoe and pulled Valentine to a table.

*Geez. Hormonal women were touchy.*

Stanley waved me over. "I'm Babette'th manager," he lisped. "Kate might be right about the chocolateth being from Than Franthithco. We don't carry Ghirardelli at Higgly Piggly."

Zelda smacked his arm. "If you decide to sell 'em, I've got your sample girl." She gestured at me. "Frenchie here is perfect."

There was no point in correcting her. She couldn't process my name, so it was pointless to tell her that a woman called Frenchie should represent mustard, not Italian chocolate.

My phone rang. It was my parents' number, so I let it go to voicemail. Calls from home were often as deadly as this party.

The ringing resumed.

My parents again. I declined the call.

My text tone pinged, and I frowned at the message. *Pick up, Francesca. I'm your mother. I know when you're avoiding me.*

As long as I lived, I'd never understand how the woman did that.

On the next ring, I answered. "Mom, I'm working, okay?"

"That's no way to talk to your mother, dear," she shrilled. "And I called Bradley, so I know you're on a girls' trip in Niagara Falls."

Apparently, I needed to remind my fiancé not to out my location to anyone, especially my family. "Why did you call Bradley?"

"You didn't answer. What was I supposed to do?"

"Try me later? Leave a message? Wait for me to call you back?"

"What for? You're not at work."

I sat at the bar to keep from literally kicking myself for not getting a drink before I cut everyone off.

My mother gave her signature long-suffering sigh. "Bradley said you're at a bachelorette party. Too bad."

The party *was* bad, but she couldn't know that. "What do you mean?"

"You remember the old saying, 'always a bachelorette party, never a bridal shower?'"

"No, because it's 'always a bridesmaid, never a bride.'"

"You would know, Francesca. You were just a bridesmaid...again."

It was a low blow to bring my best friend Veronica's wedding into this, but it wasn't the lowest she'd sunk. As part of a cocka-mamie Sicilian-American tradition to help hard-up Catholic gals land a husband, she and my nonna once made me steal a lemon from a St. Joseph's Day church altar intended to feed the poor. "Correction...I was a maid of honor. Now, what did you want, Mom?"

"Besides a happily married daughter and a grandchild?"

*If this call goes on much longer, the paramedics will have to resuscitate Amber and me both.* "Yeah," I said, deadpan, "besides that."

"Oh, it was nothing important."

My eyes rolled, and I heard a click on the line. My eyes made another round because I knew it was my eighty-one-year-old Sicilian nonna.

"Franki," she rasped in her thick accent, "who is-a this-a party for?"

"Babette Lang, but she's not here yet."

"How old is-a she?"

I hesitated. Since I was unmarried, age was a tricky topic in my family, and Babette was only a year younger than I am. "Thirty-one."

"*Mamma mia!* No wonder she's-a not at-a the party! Her knees-a probably gave-a out."

I eyed a Dora balloon that was already deflating and fervently sympathized with it. My nonna never missed a chance to remind me that I was a *zitella*, which, in Sicily, meant a life of church, prayer, and facial hair.

Shouting broke out, and I spun to see Charlie staring open-mouthed at Amber.

"Francesca?" Anxiety upped the piercing quality of my mother's voice. "Who's shouting?"

"Babette's fiancé."

Nonna chuckled. "I'll-a bet he just-a found out-a how old she is."

I motioned for Rock to pour me a drink. Between the party and this call, it was worth the risk to my life. "Oh, Babette's here," I fibbed. "*Ciao ciao!*"

Before they could protest, I hung up and slowly approached Charlie at the bar. Kate said he'd been shaken by his interaction with Amber, and Chelsea had tried to claim that it was because he was upset that she'd crashed the party. But I suspected his reaction was rooted in guilt, especially if he *was* making out with her in the elevator at his bride-to-be's bachelorette party.

Unaware that I was nearing, Charlie stole a glance at Rock, who was still trying to figure out how to make my drink. Then he slipped behind the bar and crouched in front of my suitcase.

I crept up behind him just as he reached for the zipper on the front pocket. "Can I help you with something?"

Charlie leapt and turned as red as a bottle of Campari. "Uh, no. Why?"

"Because this is my bag."

"Oh...I didn't know."

I distinctly remembered telling him it belonged to me when he'd yelled about it being in the bar. But, to give him the benefit of the doubt, the guy *was* drunk and distraught. "You're upset. Why don't you have a seat?"

He sat on a stool and rubbed his eyes.

I leaned on the counter. "Any idea what could've happened to Amber?"

"Excuse me." Charlene got up from her chair in the corner and came to the bar. "Rumor has it you're a private investigator."

I nodded. "Yes, in New Orleans."

She slammed her book on the counter. "I'll sit with my brother. Go look for another sucker to trick into a confession."

I added her to my suspect list. Not because she was surly, but because she was reading *Moby Dick*. Anyone who would willingly read a novel about a man out for revenge against a whale had to be deranged.

Rock handed me the drink, but I decided to pass. If anyone had slipped Amber a mickey, it was him. He'd been serving her drinks, and he hadn't lifted a girly-gloved finger to break her fall. Of course, he'd claimed that he was trying to protect his hands. *But was he? Or did he have it in for Amber for some reason?*

A possible answer hit me like, well, a *rock*. Amber could've been his ex, and if so, he might've been angry about her coming to the party to try to win back Charlie. Even if the pair didn't have a past, Rock was handsome, so they might've had a present —as in, he might've been the man I'd seen her making out with in the elevator. He'd entered the room right after I got to the party.

Rock picked up the soda gun and poured a Coke. He raised the glass to his lips.

I frowned. "I wouldn't drink that if I were you."

He spat the soda back into the glass and dabbed his tongue with a bar towel.

Not only did the guy not know how to mix cocktails, he also didn't know how poison worked. "So, what was Amber drinking?"

"Vodka martinis, dirty."

"Anyone else have vodka?"

He tapped his forehead, probably trying to jumpstart his brain. "Chelsea and Charlie had screwdrivers."

Then it was probably safe. "What about vermouth?"

"Never heard of him."

I cocked my jaw. "How long did you say you've been a bartender?"

"This is my third gig."

"And an uptight perfectionist like Chelsea hired you?"

He pulled up a glove. "I lied on my résumé, all right? I need the money for a hand-modeling portfolio."

"Lied on your résumé." My eyes narrowed to the width of a

cocktail sword. "What else are you lying about, Rock? Your relationship with Amber?"

His chin receded into his neck. "Whoa. I didn't know private eyes could see in people's brains."

My brows shot up for a couple of reasons. But mainly because I hadn't expected the hand model to tip his hand. "When was that? Before or after Charlie?"

"During, but I broke it off after an hour. She has a freaky fetish."

*That could be relevant to my investigation.* "What is it?"

"She kept wanting to hold my hand."

Rock wasn't as dumb as a rock, he was as dumb as a box of rocks—shipping-container sized.

Merry ushered a male and female paramedic into the room and led them to Amber's body. They were joined by Kate and Valentine, and after a brief exchange the paramedics began tending to Amber.

Merry joined me at the bar. "Mo's back at the reception desk, and he won't be leaving his post." She gave me a knowing look. "I had a spare pair of zip ties in my bag."

*Zip ties? What kind of Girl Scouts was she in charge of?*

"Also," she glanced at Rock, "when I talked to the paramedics, I mentioned how stiff Amber's torso was, and do you know what the woman said?" She tapped her breastbone. "Wooden chest syndrome."

"Is that like when your silicone implants harden?"

Merry spread her arms. "Do I look like I have implants?"

She definitely didn't, but I wasn't going to say so. Based on the faces she'd been making at her phone throughout the party, I was a little concerned about her. "Then what is it?"

"A symptom of opioid toxicity."

I pulled out my cell and googled *wooden chest syndrome*. I got almost two million hits, and all of them referenced opioids, including Fentanyl. "That puts a different spin on her death.

Amber could've accidentally offed herself with a prescription drug."

"My experience tells me it's foul play."

I started to ask what experience she was referring to, but then I remembered—those hooligan Girl Scouts.

Merry turned on her barstool and surveyed the guests. "And if I'm right, we certainly don't lack suspects."

I couldn't argue with her there. I'd never seen a bigger bunch of potential felons, not even the night I spent in New Orleans Central Lockup. "Whatever happened to Amber, someone needs to tell Babette."

"She's probably still passing out wieners at the Falls, thanks to that awful boss of hers."

"You handled Mo, so I'll deal with Stanley." I ambled to the end of the bar where Babette's bald boss was chatting up Zelda. "Hey, given what's happened, it's time for the guest of honor to come to her party."

"I wish she would," Stanley gushed. "She should've left the Falls by now, but no one'th theen or heard from her. Why do you think I'm drinking?"

I'd assumed it was because he was having to watch Zelda gum her food. "Have you tried calling her?"

"I jutht did, but it went right to voicemail. Even happened an hour ago when the manager on duty at Higgly Piggly called to remind her to drop off the wiener cothtume, per policy. She hathn't returned the call, and the thtore is liable."

Zelda gave his hand a squeeze. "Don't worry, Stanley. Babette's a professional. She'll turn in that costume, you watch."

"Let'th hope." He wiped his bare head with a bar nap. "She *did* leave her party dreth at the thtore."

*Her dress? Something wasn't right.* "Did anyone see her leave the Falls?"

"That'th the funny thing. The café manager thaid no one thaw her go." Stanley's hand shook as he reached for his glass. "The management at Higgly Piggly is ruthleth. They'll have my head on a platter if that cothtume doethn't show up." His gaze fell on Zelda like an axe on a tree stump. "Next, they'll have yourth."

She pulled her wig low on her forehead. "How much did you say it costs to replace one of those wiener getups?"

My guess was no more than her hair and teeth combined, but I didn't listen to Stanley's answer. I was too busy processing the ramifications of what I'd learned.

Amber was dead, and Babette was missing. *Were the two things related?*

It didn't make sense that no one had seen a woman in a wiener costume leaving the Falls, unless...

What I was thinking was so shocking that I grabbed the soda gun and splashed my face with water.

*Was Babette dead, too?*

# VALENTINE

## ARLENE MCFARLANE

This wasn't good. A dead body. A missing bachelorette. Everyone pointing fingers at everyone. Plus, I could tell by the way Kate pulled me away to a table that she wasn't thrilled with Franki's remark about Kate being in her room with Babette's fiancé.

"Can you believe that woman?" Kate planted her hands on her hips. "Saying I'm some cheap floozy?"

We watched Franki spritz her face with the soda gun, give a total body shake, then, in full control, swipe her beautiful mane off her shoulders and meander over to the next suspect. I liked how this tall woman operated.

"I don't think she meant anything by it," I said to Kate, waiting for my stomach to settle after seeing Amber drop dead. "Speaking as someone who's often put her foot in her mouth, I have a feeling Franki just jumped to conclusions."

"You're probably right, but I'll feel better once I can prove those chocolates are the ones I brought from San Francisco. And who is Franki to point fingers? *She* was the one with the suspicious-looking luggage. Obvious by how Charlie flipped out when he saw it."

This was true. It seemed as if Charlie had recognized the suitcase, but if so, who did he think it belonged to? My best guess was Babette. I knew she hauled one of those hard-shelled, rounded-edged pharmaceutical bags around with her, and Franki's had the same look. I glanced around the room. Was there anyone else a bag like this could belong to?

Candace was gobbling cream puffs at a corner table, ignoring the rule about food and drink being off limits. The suitcase couldn't have belonged to her unless broomsticks had saddlebags for carting luggage. Plus, Candace swooped in *after* the luggage debacle.

I took a deep breath and ordered myself to lay off the mean thoughts toward Candace. I was naturally a cheery, friendly person. Okay, clearly I had a sassy streak. But giving Candace digs was just plain unbecoming. Besides, I had more important things to think about.

The paramedics were waiting on the arrival of the ME to officially pronounce Amber dead, and approaching sirens said the cops were almost here. I was formulating a plan that might answer my own questions when I caught Stanley hop off his barstool and strut up to six-foot-one Rock, head tilted up, lips pursed, like he was Jack surmising how he was going to climb the beanstalk.

"I don't know what happened to thith Amber woman." Stanley pointed his stubby finger at Rock's chest. "But I have a thneaking thuthpicion *you* know what happened to *Babette*."

His agitation seemed to worsen as the night wore on, but it didn't have any effect on Rock. He looked down at Stanley and rammed his lime-green-gloved hands on his trim hips. "Why would *I* know what happened to Babette?"

Stanley widened his stance, his ill-fitted jacket sliding around on his shoulders. I had to give him credit. He wasn't the least bit intimidated by Rock's size. "Becauth you were jealouth about

Babette getting a commercial role as the wiener. I know darn well you wanted that part."

Zelda jumped down from her barstool, landing square on her scuffed pumps, then paraded up to the men, arms swinging, bangles clanking. "Now, Stanley. What makes you think Rock was upset about not getting that role?"

Stanley shrugged her off. "You weren't at the thet the day Rock thtumbled in drunk, making crude thlurth at Babette."

"So what if I did?" Rock thrust his muscular pecs forward.

"I thaw you lurking around the deli counter earlier today while Babette wathn't watching. Nobody'th theen hide nor hair of her since she left work. Were you waiting for her to finish her shift in order to *kidnap* her? Put an end to her role ath the wiener?"

"*Pff.*" Rock waved him away with a nervous finger flutter, his eyes skittering across the room, probably hoping no one else was catching their exchange.

Unfortunately for him, Kate and I were tuned to the conversation, her wide eyes fastened on me while I peeked past her shoulder at the threesome.

"You got Rock all wrong, Stanley." Zelda barked out a nasty cough, then gasped for air.

Careful not to touch her with his prize-winning gloved hands, Rock angled down at her, a questioning look in his eyes. "You okay, Zelda?" He peeked from Amber's stiff body back to his agent. "You didn't, uh, eat anything funny, did you?"

The trio swiveled to Candace downing pastries like there was no tomorrow, and if the food *was* poisoned, there was a good possibility there wouldn't be.

Zelda wheezed, flapping her hand up and down. "Nah. I'm fine. I need another cigarette is all." She barked so hard again, the force of her cough shifted her wig off center. "Listen, Stanley. Just put that bee back in your bonnet. Rock's been here most of the day, right, Rock?"

"Uh, yeah."

"See? He's not interested in Babette. In fact, we're holding out for a deal with Ball Park Franks. That'll make him a household name."

Stanley narrowed his eyes on both of them. "Humph. Good luck with that." He stormed to the other side of the room, plunked down at Candace's table, and popped one of her cream puffs into his mouth.

Hmm. This exchange promised to be fun, but God didn't give me an eye for detail to miss what else was going on in the room.

Merry and Franki had things under control with the paramedics, thank goodness. I'd been around enough corpses to know dead when I saw it, and Amber's chocolate-smeared blue lips and bare nails the shade of Revlon's Sultry Blue nail enamel told me she wouldn't be rejoining the party any time soon. Fortunately, she was getting plenty of attention from everyone else.

Kate excused herself to use the bathroom, and I roamed to the bar. I set my bag on the stool next to Charlene who had her back to me, babysitting her brother while keeping a hawk eye on Franki.

In case Charlene accused me of snooping—which I was—I whipped out my compact mirror and pretended to carefully reapply my lipstick. In reality, I could hit my target blindfolded and standing on my head. I was more interested in Charlene's book lying on the bar.

*Moby Dick*? Egad. I almost swiped my frosted lipstick across my cheek. Hold on! What was that written on her bookmark? I tipped closer, compact mirror to my nose, squinting as I read the word Fen-tan-yl.

*Fentanyl!* Every muscle in my body tensed. Why in the world would Charlene have the name of an opioid scribbled on a bookmark crammed inside a novel? I leaned past the bar at the mob surrounding Amber on the floor. Was the drug somehow involved in her death? The foamy mouth and blue lips already implied this wasn't an ordinary passing.

I peered at Chelsea on her knees, smoothing Amber's limp hair, covertly dabbing the foam clustered at the sides of her mouth. What was she trying to do? Wipe away the evidence before anyone noticed? Or was she just trying to be helpful?

"Please, miss." The paramedic reached out an arm, signaling for Chelsea to back up.

She got to her feet, and it struck me that Merry had said she was a pharmacist. Well now, that was interesting. We had a pharmacist who knew about drugs, and a sister who was toting a book around with *Fentanyl* written on her bookmark. Did Chelsea recommend Charlene take Fentanyl for some reason, maybe as pain relief for an upcoming surgery? Or was this something else? Something more sinister, like using the drug to cause an overdose...

From what I could tell, Charlene wasn't thrilled about being here, and she didn't seem to like anyone in the room. But did she have a real hate-on for Amber? Enough to kill her?

I was getting ahead of myself. After all, there were no drugs found anywhere, and I was certain that if Amber had been popping pills in the bathroom when she'd been in there with Kate, Kate would've mentioned this. For all I knew, the name written on Charlene's bookmark could mean a number of things. Maybe she needed to pick up the drug for a relative. Maybe Fentanyl was the name of a medical thriller and the next book she wanted to read. Maybe she—

Kate pulled me away from the bar, having returned from the ladies' room. "Look at Charlene giving daggers to Franki. Protecting her brother like he's King Tut."

I slid my compact back in my bag and swiveled around to Charlie who seemed a bit pale. "With the amount of booze he's been consuming, he might end up like King Tut, mummified and all."

Kate smiled at that, then nodded at my empty soda glass. "At least you and I won't end up like him."

"Nope." I shuddered. "Liquor and I have a love-hate relationship. It loves going down, but I hate the effect after even a teaspoon—or peastoon, which is how I'd slur it with a drunken smile while guys like Stanley suddenly turn into hunks like Bradley Cooper."

Kate giggled, eyes back on Charlene. "I don't know about her. Charlene's very strange. Like who reads a book at a bachelorette party? I guess when you're a librarian it's not so weird."

"A *librarian.*" Hmm. Maybe that was why she had *Fentanyl* scribbled on her bookmark. Doing research for work, perhaps?

Merry strolled over, giving the room a once-over. "How are you enjoying things *now?*"

I nodded toward Candace in her red hooker outfit, feeding Stanley another cream puff. "I thought Candace crashing the party was going to be the highlight. I guess Amber dropping dead topped that." My hand flew to my mouth. "Oops. Did I just say that? Sorry."

Merry gave a relaxed wave. "No need to apologize. I always tell my Girl Scouts to be prepared. But how could any of us have been prepared for *this*? I mean, wooden chest syndrome? Who knew that was a symptom of opioid toxicity."

"Not me." I swallowed, thankful I was facing this with these supportive friends.

I shared what Kate and I'd overheard between Rock and Stanley, adding my Fentanyl discovery written on Charlene's bookmark.

Merry made an *O* with her mouth. "This isn't good."

"I'm still trying to figure out how Amber got those chocolates," Kate said. "I'm *sure* they're the ones I brought from home."

I licked my lips, the taste of my vanilla-scented lipstick comforting me. "I have an idea. I want to check Babette's room. See if there's anything that explains her absence. Kate, you want to come and look for the chocolates? Maybe the ones Amber ate were from an identical box."

"With a replica of a San Francisco cable car and the Golden Gate Bridge?"

"Good point. But we won't know for sure unless we do some snooping."

"I'm in." Kate rubbed her hands fiendishly, which was pretty cute. Usually she was rubbing her belly.

"What do you want me to do?" Merry asked. "And if you say, 'Go find your clipboard,' I'll scream."

I grinned, my gutsy side resurfacing, squashing the anxiety that had been building all night. "You've got enough to oversee here, but let's all exchange phone numbers. If the cops arrive and for any reason decide to search Babette's room, give us a heads-up so we can vacate the area."

"Good idea. And here's Franki's. I got hers earlier. I'll slip her yours while you're gone."

The three of us covertly tapped our phones, then tucked them away.

Following a deep breath, I hitched my bag over my shoulder and nodded at Kate. "Ready?"

She squared her shoulders. "As I'll ever be."

"Great. First, let's hit Mo at the front desk for the key."

Merry raised a finger in the air. "He might be a little indisposed at the moment."

"The zip ties?" I asked, having overheard Merry's report to Franki earlier.

"Yep. I knew those things would come in handy."

"I like how you think. And no worries. I've got it covered."

Kate and I bobbed past a deflating Dora the Explorer balloon and slunk out of the party room, picking up our pace as we strutted down the hall. It felt like we were a couple of hotshot cops you see in the movies, walking in slow motion, shoulder to shoulder, confident faces, arms swinging widely. Where was the *Mission Impossible* music when you needed it?

I shared my key-snatching plan with Kate on the way to the front desk, and she gave a thumbs-up, followed by an immediate tug on my arm. "Wait. Can I slip into the bathroom first? The babies are sitting right on my bladder."

There went the *Mission Impossible* music. "Sure." I smiled. "I'll wait here."

She slipped into the bathroom, and I checked my phone again, thinking there was a chance Babette had texted or left a message. Nothing.

Only a text from Romero. *Miss you.*

This was meant in more ways than one, and heat rushed through me, my legs suddenly weak as if Romero were standing here, undressing me with his dangerously sexy eyes.

I gulped at the hunger in those words, then sent him a light-hearted smoochie-kiss emoji. I stuffed my phone back in my bag as Kate rejoined me. *Whew.* Not a moment too soon.

A second later, we were standing at the front desk, staring down at Mo using his chin to move the computer mouse back and forth.

"Uh, Mo? What are you doing?"

He gave me a miserable look. "What do you think I'm doing?" He swung halfway around, displaying the zip ties clenching his wrists. "I can't even turn up the volume on *Weekend at Bernie's* with *these* shackling me. And it's getting to a good part, too."

I sidled up behind the counter in my sparkly heels. "Let me help you with that."

"No!" He leaped off his stool and flung his back to the wall. "Stay away from me."

"You poor thing." I laid on the sympathy with a trowel. When dealing with someone as slimy as Mo, attitude was everything. "I can take those zip ties off you."

"No. You people are all *crazy*. First, that drunk, Charlie, bribes me with a pizza pocket to give him a key to your no-show bachelorette's room. Then there's a murder."

"Nobody said it was murder," Kate clarified, though we shared a look that implied we knew different.

"Wait a minute," I said to Mo. "You let Charlie into Babette's room?"

"He said he had chocolates for her. Honestly, the guy's a moron. Had to tell him ten times, room 418. Then he didn't take both keys. Policy is every guest gets two keys. The other one's right here, too." He dropped back on his stool beside a key card envelope marked 418.

"If that didn't take the cake," he went on, "that Girl Scout leader from Iowa did *this* to me. *Zip ties!*" he said bitterly, the garlic on his breath wafting into the air.

"Maybe she was practicing a new maneuver for her troop."

He gaped at me like I was on something. "She has it in for me. Told me if I so much as moved away from my desk without these on, she'd hunt me down. Said it with a carefree smile on her face, too, blonde curls bouncing like Shirley Temple. But she didn't fool me."

I grinned inside at Merry's chutzpah, recalling a similar stunt I'd once pulled to stop a blind date and his wandering hands. Okay, so I'd "accidentally" spilled peroxide on his lap to reinforce my point instead of tying him with zip ties. It was important to use what was at one's disposal.

Mo looked from Kate to me. "I run a nice, quiet hotel here. No issues. No complaints. Then you lot come in, and suddenly there's a dead body, paramedics crawling all over, and—*aaah!*" He jumped off his stool again. "The cops!"

We turned in time to see he wasn't kidding. The uniforms rushed in, asked where the victim was, and ran in the direction we pointed. Amid the commotion, I angled over the lower part of the counter and unsuccessfully tried to sweep up the card.

Mo let out a weary sigh, falling back on his seat. "This isn't my night." Then, realizing I was still standing at the counter, he squinted at me, the sweat on his upper lip adding to the grease already there. "I could get in a lot of trouble with you back here. This area is for staff only."

"Just trying to help." I raised my palms in the air. "But if you don't want my assistance…"

"*Uhhhhh!*" On cue, Kate lurched forward on the other side of the desk, hands gripping her belly.

"What is it?" Mo popped up so fast, he was starting to resemble a jack-in-the-box.

"I think it's…*uhhhhh*," she moaned again, legs buckling to the floor. "Labor pains."

I slid the key in my bag and bolted around the desk. "You okay?"

She leaned on me as I helped her to her feet, then took a heavy breath. "I think so. If I can just make it to my room I'll be fine."

I hurried her down the hall, arm around her waist, heels clicking swiftly on the floor.

"What about me?" Mo piped on the balls of his feet, arms clasped behind his back.

"I'll tell Merry you're asking for her," I called over my shoulder.

We whipped around the corner to the elevators and simultaneously bent over, laughing so hard I was afraid I was going to pee my pants. I didn't know how Kate was holding it in.

"You got the key, right?" she asked.

I pulled it out of my bag. "You bet. Now to get to her room before anyone else thinks of it."

A moment later, we stepped off the elevator and hustled down the hall to 418. I slipped the key in the slot and nothing happened. I tried it the other way. Zilch. "Shoot. Maybe he didn't program this one. That's happened to me before."

"What are we going to do?" Kate asked.

I dropped my bag to the floor and rummaged through it until I found my own room key. I ripped off a piece of magnetic nail tape that I always carried with me—after all you never knew when you might need a quick fix—and placed it on the back of the card.

"What's that for?" Kate knelt beside me.

My heart was pounding like bongo drums, alerting me that we could be caught at any time. But I couldn't stop now. I was doing this for Babette.

I dug out my ultra-thin metal nail file attached to my nail clippers, and a bobby pin from the depths of my bag, then rose to my feet. "I once escaped from a locked sauna with nothing but these tools and a lot of luck. It wasn't a door like this, but what have we got to lose?"

I went to work, guiding the key into the slot, wiggling the bobby pin and nail file through the gap at the bottom. I finagled with it until my fingertips were sore and my forehead was drenched in sweat. *Darn*. This was like painting my nails with crayons for all the good it did.

I had one more trick up my sleeve before giving up. I scratched off the plastic nib on the tip of the bobby pin, then dipped the bobby pin in my Wahl hair clipper oil.

"Kate, I want you to hold the card in the slot. When I say *go*, push it up and slide it back an eighth of an inch, okay?"

She gave a rapid head bob up and down, steadying her hands on the card.

"Go."

She lifted the card and brought it back slightly. At the same time, I wormed the bobby pin to the left while tickling the nail file a fraction to the right. A tense moment passed, then suddenly we heard a faint *click*, and a green light flashed before us.

Kate's eyes brightened, and she did a hop on the spot. "We did it?"

I was as shocked as she was. "Looks like it." I pushed down the handle, and the door opened.

"Wait till Jim hears about this," she exclaimed, giving me a high five.

Yeah. Probably not something I'd share with Romero, being he was on the side of the law, and theoretically this was breaking and entering. Oh well, he wasn't here, was he?

We scurried inside, and immediately Kate gasped. "Look! I knew it. Here's the red ribbon from the chocolate box, and even the padded insert that keeps them in place." She made fists with her swollen hands. "I *knew* those were my chocolates. But why would Charlie have brought them here and then back down to the party room? And how did Amber get them? Was she in the room, too?" She turned to me. "Do you think she stole them?"

"Maybe Charlie opened them up here and then took them down to share."

I glanced from the red ribbon strewn on the bed to Kate, my heart suddenly knocking in my chest. "Suppose Charlie took them down to the party, and someone tampered with them?"

"Who would do something crazy like that?"

I shrugged, reminding her of what Merry had shared about the effects of drug poisoning on a corpse, not to mention Charlene carrying a bookmark with *Fentanyl* written on it.

"Charlene a murderer?" Kate crinkled her nose.

"I wouldn't rule her out."

We stared at each other, contemplating this, my eyes shifting from the rumpled bed cover to a dark gray piece of luggage by the window.

"Kate." I gestured to the suitcase.

She looked from the bag back to me. "Babette's pharmaceutical bag."

We dashed for the suitcase and placed it on its side. Technically, we'd already broken into the room. Why stop now? We flipped the latches, and the suitcase popped open.

Hundreds of tiny pill bottles, capsules, packets, latex gloves, syringes, and other samples looked up at us from neat little rows and slots. It was like a candy store for pharmacists.

Kate stared at Babette's name tag by the suitcase handle. "Babette must've checked in after her sales job, left her luggage here, then went to Higgly Piggly."

"True." A shiver moved through me. "There are enough drugs here to OD half the hotel, if one had the mind to. I guess this answers why Charlie freaked out when he saw Franki's luggage." I stared back inside the suitcase. "Who knows who came into this room once he had the key...or if any of these drugs played a role in Amber's death."

I grabbed a bottle labeled *Fentanyl*. "Look! Exactly what Charlene had written on her bookmark. A drug—like Merry had said —that could cause wooden chest syndrome if one were poisoned with it." I scanned the contents in the bag, my mouth suddenly dry. "You think someone is setting Babette up for murder?"

Kate shuddered at the thought. "I don't know, but I think we'd better get out of here. Our prints are all over this room."

I didn't argue. We closed the bag, wiped things down, and raced back to the party room, screeching to a stop when we saw the cops questioning guests.

I calmed my beating heart and gave Kate a sideways glance. She returned the glance, our eyes connecting. We may have stolen a hotel key, unlawfully entered Babette's room, and broken into her personal belongings. But the last thing we wanted was to announce that we'd found incriminating evidence that might declare our friend a murderer.

# BABETTE

## TRACI ANDRIGHETTI

*T*he wind picked up along the Niagara River walkway, chilly for a June night. But I didn't mind the cold. This silly hot dog costume was so thick it was too hot to wear clothes underneath. If I did, I'd end up looking like one of those shriveled gas station wieners that had been left on the warmer too long.

I pulled my phone from the pocket in the side of my hot dog bun. "Shoot. Still no signal." My service had been hit and miss since I'd been at the Falls, and it was nonexistent on the walkway because it bordered a cliff. "I'm sure Chelsea's fuming that I'm over an hour late to my own bachelorette party. But Kate and Valentine will make sure the guests are fed, and Franki will definitely keep the drinks flowing. Since she's from New Orleans, she'll have them so sloshed they probably won't even notice I'm missing."

I pocketed my phone. At least I got rid of Stanley's wienies before he went ape on me. *Rotten boss.*

I went in search of someone who could give me directions back to the parking lot. Even though it was already dark, I was sure I'd find a few tourists.

The Falls were even more beautiful at night, backlit with

colored lights. As I rounded a turn, part of the Falls came into view.

"Oh, my stars above!" I used my late grandmother's favorite exclamation because the water glowed the same shade of blue as the sapphires on her heirloom bracelet.

A pang went through my chest. I missed Grandma Barbie so much. And to think that my lowlife ex-boyfriend had stolen her bracelet the day I'd inherited it. He didn't own a thing that hadn't come from a pawnshop. I'd been pestering local pawnshop owners with pictures of the bracelet ever since, and it had finally paid off. That no-good rat had pawned it, and the shop owner had been kind enough to text me a picture. "*Ooh!*" My mouth puckered. "I should've known better than to date a guy named Johnny 'The Mooch' Muccitelli."

My fists clenched in the yellow satin opera gloves I'd put on, away from Stanley's watchful eye, to add much-needed shine to my costume. I couldn't let Grandma Barbie's precious bracelet go to a stranger. Besides, it was my something old and something blue for my wedding. "I have to get that bracelet tonight before someone buys it. My guests will understand when I explain why I was late."

Lights from the Cave of the Winds Tour ticket pavilion illuminated flights of stairs scaling the cliffside. "Maybe that's the way to the parking lot."

A short, sixty-something man exited the pavilion, waving a mass of keys. "You can't go that way, miss. The Bridal Veil is closed until tomorrow."

"The Bridal Veil?" I clasped my hands in front of my face, a coo escaping my lips. "What a lovely name for a boutique. I'm about to get married."

He smoothed the scant hair on his scalp. "Oh, it's not a boutique. It's the name of one of the three Falls."

"This is my first visit, but I thought there were only two, the American and the Canadian."

"Yeah, but ours are split in two by a rock formation. The small one at the end is called the Bridal Veil Falls." He smacked his lips and pulled up his pants. "Although it's not really small. That baby's fifty-six feet across."

I looked at the water, and the lights changed to baby pink. "First sapphire blue, and now my favorite color," I whispered. *Were the Falls sending me a sign?* "Can I please take a quick look? Since I'm getting married, it might be a bad omen if I don't."

His face softened. "Wait here." He entered the pavilion and came out with a disposable raincoat. "This'll keep your bun from getting soggy. I'll help you put it on."

"You're so kind." I was five-ten without the costume, and in it I was six-ten. The extra foot was all wiener. I bent over as much as I could to help the man, but a cage inside the costume to keep the bun and hot dog firm was making it difficult.

After a couple of attempts, he pulled the raincoat over my costume and gave a satisfied nod. "Yellow, like mustard."

I held up my hands and wiggled my fingers like I'd seen Marilyn Monroe do when she sang "Diamonds Are a Girl's Best Friend" in *Gentlemen Prefer Blondes*. "And it matches my opera gloves."

He took a step back and eyed the top of the hot dog. "The hood's not going to reach all the way to that wiener. One sec." He returned inside the pavilion and reappeared with a rain hat. "Hold still."

I bent at an incline again.

He jumped several times but couldn't reach the top of my costume. He stopped and pulled up his pants. "I was a disc-golfer back in the day, so don't be alarmed." His face grew tense, and he aimed and tossed the hat like a frisbee. It landed on the peak of my dumb wiener head on the first try.

I raised my arms. "Goal!" Just because I was mad at Stanley for making me parade around in this stupid costume all night didn't mean I had to take it out on this nice man.

His head bobbed, and he repressed a proud smile. "Yep. Still got my throwing arm."

"Before I go, can you tell me how to get to the parking lot?"

He pointed in the opposite direction. "Head back the way you came, and when you get to the grassy field, turn south. It'll take you to Goat Island Road. The lot's there on the other side."

He made it sound so easy. "Thank you, sir."

"Barney." He grinned and shoved his hands in his pockets. "And congrats to Mr. Mayer. He's one lucky dog."

I smiled, but I didn't know who he was talking about. My fiancé's last name was Miller.

"What a nice man that Barney was, giving me this raincoat." I patted my side and looked up at the spray coming off the Bridal Veil wall of water. "It'll even protect my phone from the Falls." I couldn't afford for it to get ruined, especially tonight.

I approached the stairs to the first viewing platform, but the goofy hot dog shoes were slipping out from under me. "Darn these dogs. Can't even get a grip."

Even though I hated to ruin my opera gloves, I was determined to get close to the Falls. Luckily Rock Stone had taught me the importance of protecting my hands for work. He's not as dumb as some of Zelda's other clients, like George Looney.

I grabbed hold of the railing and pulled myself up. Three feet into my climb, my hand slipped, and I shot down the rail like a log flume in the Splash Mountain ride at Disney World. I landed on my stomach and slid to a stop. "Good thing I have the extra padding on my costume, and my tummy."

Not to be defeated by a little water, I rose to my hands and knees and crawled up the steps. I made it to the viewing platform and tried to stand. My feet slid in different directions, and my arms flailed. Then I tipped over backwards like a felled tree in a forest—just before it bounced down some stairs. "Oh, no—oh—oh—oh—oh—oh—oh—oh—oh—ow!"

I pressed my lips together and watched my hat blow away,

then I glared at the Bridal Veil. "Are you trying to tell me something about my upcoming nuptials?"

A huge shot of water splashed my face. "Thanks. A lot."

Sputtering and grumbling to myself, I wiped my eyes, crawled to the edge of the platform, and managed to stand up. Best to skip the viewing platform. But I wasn't going to be deterred from taking a peek from the railing. "Marilyn did it in the movie *Niagara*, so you can do it too, Babette."

Fighting the windy force of the Falls, I slid my feet across the wood as if I were ice skating, finally making it to the closest rail.

I gazed up at the Bridal Veil. The thundering water was awe-inspiring, and it gave off so much energy. I'd heard that Native Americans believed Niagara Falls was a spiritual place. "I like those Native Americans. Such kindred spirits. And wise, too."

"Mommy, look!" a child shouted. "Can I eat it?"

I managed to pull off my raincoat and turned from the railing to a chubby boy, seven or so years of age, in his own plastic raincoat. He was eyeing me while licking his lips.

His mother took him by the arm and pulled him away. "It's not a real hot dog, Andy."

"It is too, Mommy. It's got a bun and everything."

She shot me an embarrassed smile. "We decided to sneak up here before dinner, but it's been a really long hike."

"Aw." I tossed my raincoat in a garbage bin and smiled at the boy. I hoped Charlie and I would have one just like him some day. "I believe the Cave of the Winds Snack Bar is up ahead, and I have a feeling they make a really great hot dog and fries."

Andy mouthed the words *hot dog*. Then he lowered his head and charged at me like a linebacker for the New England Patriots.

My thighs took the brunt of the blow, and my back slammed into the railing. The force was so strong that something inside my costume popped. Instinctively, I felt for my phone.

*Gone.*

Andy released my legs, and I spun toward the water in time to see the display light up as it hit the surface of the river below.

My stomach sank like the device. *Now how was I going to contact anyone?* That darn phone had cost me a not-so-small fortune.

"Yuck." Andy spat and slapped his tongue. "That hot dog tastes like Play-Doh."

My hands went to my mouth. He'd taken a big bite out of my costume foam—on my belly. I wished something I never thought I'd wish in my entire life: that I'd left on the Spanx I wore over my briefs when I made rounds to doctors' offices for my pharmaceutical sales job.

Andy's mother stooped and grabbed his hand. Her gaze landed on my naked belly button, her eyes widening to the size of the hole. "Oh." She bolted upright and pulled her son's raincoat hood over his face. "I'm so sorry."

I couldn't blame the hungry little boy. Thanks to the water from the Falls, I *did* look like I'd been roasting on a spit. "That's okay, but—"

"Come on, Andy." She dragged him by the hand.

"Hey, wait! This isn't my costume. You have to pay for the damage."

The woman hurried off with her son.

I didn't know whether they couldn't hear me over the water, or whether they were ignoring me. Either way, I was too weighed down to chase after them.

My gaze lowered to my belly button in the darkening light. "*Ooh!*" I gritted my teeth. "This costume is so cheap, it's running like panty hose." I couldn't risk exposing myself, even if it was dark out. I tried to pull the bun over the hole, but it was sewn into place, and it only made the hole bigger.

"Ouch." Something inside the costume, like a broken coat hanger, stabbed my stomach. I removed one of my wet opera gloves and slipped my arm inside the costume. "A broken wire!

Gosh. Even the metal is third rate." I took my fingers and bent the wire forward, away from my skin. I slipped my arm back out, and the wire boinged through the wiener.

"Oh, geez. Stanley is going to kill me, and then when I'm dead, he's still going to make me pay for a new costume." I pulled on my glove and started walking the way I'd come, trying to figure out how I was going to pay for a costume, a phone, and my grandma's bracelet, not to mention the wedding.

A rustling of bushes startled me from my worries. I stopped in my tracks as an old man with a long beard like a billy goat's gruff climbed from the river embankment with a fishing pole and a bucket.

He gave me the once-over and kicked up his heels. "Hot diggity dog!"

I lowered my hot diggity dog and speed-walked past him. I needed to find the Wienermobile, and quick.

After a few minutes, I came upon a group of teens walking toward me. One of them was smoking a cigarette, which gave me the perfect solution to my costume dilemma. I could burn the foam to close up the hole.

I sashayed up to them as if I were dressed in one of my irresistible, shapely gowns instead of this poor excuse for a costume. Remembering to always start with a polite smile, I put on a bright face and purred, "Hello. You wouldn't, by any chance, give a girl a light?"

They glanced at each other, lips tight, but their smirks and dismissive attitudes didn't get by me.

"Hooligans," I muttered. "Ignoring me like that and walking away."

I rubbed my forehead and another idea came to me. *My gloves. They're soaked anyway.* I peeled them off one by one and stuffed them in the hole. "That should hold until I get to the Wienermobile."

I came to the grassy field and cut across. Inevitably, my mind drifted to my money problems. I should've told Stanley I couldn't pass out wieners on the night of my bachelorette party, but I needed the extra cash. With all the wedding costs, my pharmaceutical sales salary had been stretched to the breaking point—make that the shattering point. Charlie had offered to pay half, but so far he hadn't given me a cent. I was starting to wonder whether Charlie Miller was another Johnny "The Mooch" Muccitelli. *Was that what the Bridal Veil Falls were saying with that splash of cold water?*

"No, that's silly. Charlie's a sweetheart." Just today he'd come to my office and offered to check in to the hotel for me to save me time. I'd refused and reminded him that my bachelorette party was off limits to the groom-to-be. But Charlie was just trying to help. He knew how hard I'd been working to convince doctors to use Fentanyl in their practices. If they agreed, I'd get a big bonus that would cover my debts. Otherwise, I had to hope that Zelda came through with a real acting job instead of another grocery store samples gig.

A Parking sign shined in the distance.

"Thank goodness. That's where I parked the Wienermobile."

I slogged through the field to the stoplight at Goat Island Road and pressed the button at the pedestrian crossing.

A young guy in a black Camaro honked his horn. "Lookin' hot, dog!"

I flashed him a dazzling smile. "Jerk," I muttered through my teeth.

A white VW Bug came to a crawl, and a surly-looking girl with purple lips and heavily lined eyes leaned out. "What a loser!"

I gasped. "I'm not a loser, I'm a wiener. I mean, winner."

She sped away, laughing out the window at me.

"So rude," I said under my breath. And it kind of hurt my feelings.

A blue truck slowed, and the driver gawked at me while twisting his handlebar mustache.

I'd had enough. "Haven't you ever seen a costume before?"

"Not a hot dog with udders." He smirked and peeled off.

"What's he talking about?" I looked down. The fingers of one of my opera gloves were hanging from the hole like a cow's udder.

The light finally changed color. *Thank God!* I yanked out the gloves, covered the opening with my hand, and with as much dignity as I could muster, I crossed the road, head held high.

The parking area was enormous. I'd been in such a hurry to get to the Falls I couldn't remember where I'd parked. If Stanley had gotten me the regular-sized Wienermobile like I'd asked instead of the Mini Cooper version, it would've stood out. *Tightwad. Never wanted to make waves—only money.*

After plodding through a sea of cars, I spotted the tail end of the wiener, gleaming in the glow of a light as if it had come straight from a boiling pot.

I pulled the key from my pocket, unlocked the door, and climbed behind the wheel—well, all of me but my head. I stuck *that* out the window because of the extra foot of wiener. *Darn Stanley!*

"Next up, the pawnshop." I slid the key into the ignition. "I can get my bracelet and use their phone to call Chelsea and let her know I'm on my way."

Humming the Oscar Mayer wiener song, I fastened my seat belt. Then I heard a loud engine and stared, as stiff as a frozen hot dog, through the windshield.

A black armored vehicle had blocked me in, and men in body armor and helmets were bounding out and surrounding my car.

"Police!" An officer aimed a submachine gun at my head. "Hands on the wheel!"

My mouth dropped in shock at the sight of their uniforms, weapons, and rock-hard muscles.

"Me?" I touched my chest—after sticking it out a little.

"I said hands on the wheel!"

"Well, you don't have to be so mean about it." I did as he said, even though they obviously had me confused with someone else, just like that nice man, Barney, at the ticket pavilion who'd thought I was marrying a Mr. Mayer.

The officer kept his gun trained on my head. "I'm going to count to ten and then approach the car. Make one move toward that fuse on your stomach, and we'll shoot."

"Fuse?" My eyes lowered to my abdomen. "Are you talking about this wire?"

"Bomb squad!" Another officer shouted into his helmet mic. "We need backup, *stat*. That hot dog report wasn't a teen prank. She's wired and ready to eat—uh, blow."

*Oh my gosh. This is a S.W.A.T. team, and they think I'm a terrorist!*

# KATE

## DIANA ORGAIN

 **o Do:**

1. See Niagara Falls.
2. ~~Does this hotel have a spa?~~
3. Hotel definitely does NOT have spa. Find spa!
4. Figure out what happened to Amber.
5. Where is Babette?

BACK IN THE PARTY ROOM, the paramedics had wheeled Amber out in a rush, and the guests were squawking about in a frenzy. I found an overstuffed chair in a dark corner of the hotel lobby and propped up my feet on a striped ottoman.

Mo, the front desk clerk, was missing. I absently wondered where he was, but took advantage of the quiet to catch my breath.

I pulled out my phone and scrolled frantically for a message from Babette. There was nothing.

I fired off a text. *Where are you?*

I fruitlessly waited for a response.

Across the empty lobby, I spotted Charlie near the doorway. He staggered toward the front desk, thought better of it, then turned and headed in my direction.

"Hey, Charlie," I called.

He stopped short and straightened, then squinted. "Hello?"

I waved at him. "It's me, Kate."

*Please don't make me get up, you jerk.*

Charlie stumbled forward. "Oh yeah. Hi, Katey."

I gritted my teeth. It wasn't worth the trouble to correct him.

In the dim light of my private nook, I could see his eyes were not only bloodshot from alcohol, but they looked swollen as if he'd been crying.

I begrudgingly took my foot off the ottoman and patted it for him.

He collapsed so urgently on it, it tipped dangerously backwards. His shirt was completely untucked, and he reeked of booze.

"Whoa, Nelly!" he said. "Someone stop the boat. I want to get off."

"Need coffee?" I asked.

He cradled his head. "No. I don't need coffee. I need *her*."

I thought for a moment. "Any idea where she is?"

He frowned and suddenly looked confused.

"I know she had to work late tonight," I said, "but I would've thought she'd be here by now."

Charlie nodded in agreement, looking like a lost puppy. "Yes, Babette should've been here by now."

"Have you heard from her?" I pressed.

"No."

After an awkward silence, I asked, "Charlie, what was Amber doing with the box of chocolates I gave you for Babette?"

"I think I'm going to puke."

I couldn't tell if he was serious or if it was just a ploy to evade the question.

*He's not green.*

Taking my chances, I repeated the question. "Do you know how Amber got hold of the chocolates?"

He pressed a hand to his forehead. "Does it matter?"

"It might."

"Amber's my ex. Was...is that true?" he gasped. "How can she be dead?"

I bit my lip. It felt in poor taste to press Charlie on the chocolates while he was processing the shock. His grief looked real.

I shifted.

And yet, if he were really grieving, he'd want to get to the bottom of what had happened to Amber.

"How did she get the chocolates, Charlie?" I asked.

He shrugged. "I really don't know. I put them in Babette's room. I don't know how Amber would even know about them. Did you mention the chocolates to her?"

"No. Why would I? I gave them to you for Babette."

His chest puffed like a peacock. "Well, I don't know. You could've talked to her about them. You two were pretty chummy earlier."

"We went to the ladies' room together—"

"Yeah. Why do y'all do that?"

"That's irrelevant," I snipped.

"Why's that? You the only one who gets to ask questions? My ex is dead, and my fiancée is missing. And for some reason I don't know half the guest list. Who are you guys? That French lady—"

"Who?"

"Frenchie!"

"Franki?"

He waved an impatient hand. "Whatever. Zelda said her name was Frenchie. Have you talked to Zelda? You're a PI, right?"

"I'm working on getting my license," I clarified.

"You should talk to her. She hated Amber. If Amber's cause of death isn't natural…"

I squinted at him. "What makes you think her death wouldn't be from natural causes?"

"Amber was in top physical shape." He practically leered. "Not an ounce of fat on her figure." He gave me a sidelong look.

*I'm pregnant, you idiot!*

I dug my fingernails into my hand to keep from screaming at him.

He snickered. "Oh. I didn't mean you…I was thinking Ba…" He bolted upright and almost toppled himself again.

"What's wrong?" I asked.

"She's not here, right? I mean. She totally hated Amber…and I left the chocolates in her room. Do you think she came back to the hotel and none of us saw her?"

The hair on my neck stood up. "I doubt it."

He made a face. "You buy that story her stupid boss is spreading? That he made her work late on the night of her own bachelorette party?"

It *was* odd. All of it was odd.

Charlie slithered back onto the ottoman, his eyes heavy. Suddenly he lurched forward and flung his arms out to the side as if losing his balance.

Goodness, I'd give him about three more minutes until he passed out from alcohol consumption.

I poked him. "Hey, what were you going to tell me about Zelda?"

"Wha'?"

"You said Zelda hated Amber. Why?"

He snorted. "Oh yeah. Zelda is Babette's talent agent. She gets 15 percent of all Babette's gigs. She had a St. Paddy's day thing all lined up for her. Babette was going to be the national St. Paddy's girl." He smirked. "She actually looks pretty hot in green. Go Irish."

I socked his arm.

"Ouch," he squealed.

"Focus! What does that have to do with Zelda hating Amber?"

He rubbed his arm. "There was a lot of dough on the line for that gig. They wanted to put Babette's face on all the merchandising stuff. It was gonna be a huge payday for us. Then somehow Amber found out about it, and Babette lost the gig. Cost Zelda a hefty sum."

"I'm not following. How exactly is Amber responsible for Babette losing the gig?"

"She called the commissioner of the parade and told them Babette wasn't Babette O'Conner, but just plain Babette Lang. Zelda got in trouble for lying about Babette's last name. In the end, Babette had to take the grocery store job, because she needed money for..." his voice broke off. "For our wedding. She wanted..." He hung his head.

I patted his shoulder. If I wasn't careful, Charlie was about to become an inconsolable drunk.

"Why did Amber do that, Charlie? Why would she care if Babette got the St. Paddy's girl gig?"

He sighed. "Amber hated Babette. She couldn't stand the thought of anything going right for her."

"Amber told me she hated you, too, Charlie. Why did she hate you?"

Charlie pulled a face as if I'd offended him. "She didn't hate me," he slurred, then scratched his head, teetering from side to side.

I watched him carefully. His pupils were dilated and he was definitely drunk. I thought of Amber. She'd been slurring her words, too.

*Just before she dropped dead.*

"Charlie, how much have you had to drink?"

"Too much," he grumbled, gripping his head. "Oh God! She's

dead!" He let out a jagged cry, then swiped at his nose with the back of his hand. "What if they arrest Babette?"

"No one is arresting Babette," I said. "She's not even here."

He frowned and looked generally confused, then stood. "If you say so. Will you go talk to Zelda? I'm going to go puke."

He spun around on a heel and staggered out of the lobby.

I straightened and fortified myself as I headed toward the ballroom. I needed to find Zelda and get answers, but something was bothering me.

*Could Babette really be here?*

Could she have snuck in without any of us seeing her?

I thought back to her room and the pharmaceutical bag...

No, it was impossible. I may not have seen Babette in a while, but there was no way she was a murderer.

Down the hallway, through the ballroom door, I could see Merry talking in an animated fashion with Valentine and Franki.

Oh, dear!

With those three girls together, there was sure to be investigation talk, and I didn't want to miss a single update.

I waddled toward the party room as fast as my wide baby load would allow!

# MERRY

## LESLIE LANGTRY

*T*he phrase "drawing the short straw" sometimes felt like a metaphor for my career in the CIA, especially when I was working with a team. Who drew the short straw in Russia and had to infiltrate a Mafia den as a singing penguin gram? This gal. Who had pulled the short toothpick in Japan and had to mud wrestle Otan the Okinawan Ox for the Yakuza's amusement? Me. Who had drawn the short straw in Chechnya and had to tell the strongman leader that his favorite gerbil had died? That's right, me again.

To be fair, it wasn't totally my fault. I had no idea that a goat would eat a gerbil. I just thought Azlan would like having a photo of his favorite gerbil on the back of his favorite goat. Well, favorite *gerbil-eating* goat. The picture turned out great, though. I got a shot of the goat and gerbil looking at each other just before...well, you know.

Chelsea sat at the bar, glaring daggers at everyone around her. It wouldn't surprise me if she could kill someone with a look. I knew an MI6 agent who could do that. He had these eyeglasses that, when activated by looking in a certain direction, could...oh wait. That's classified. It really is pretty cool, though.

Once again, I'd drawn the short straw, figuratively speaking, which meant that it was my job to talk to Charlie's sisters. Chelsea and Charlene seemed to think that rabid hostility was an emotion best reserved for fun things, like bachelorette parties.

I wasn't afraid. I'd faced way worse odds—whether it was taking on three Russian spies in a Bangkok alley to what was predicted to be a suicide mission at a Bolivian bowling alley. By the way, did you know you can kill a man with a bowling shoe? The trick is in how you use the shoelace.

Besides, aside from the copy of *Moby Dick* (which I was fairly certain Charlene didn't realize could be a useful weapon), they weren't really armed.

Steeling myself by swiping a bottle of wine off someone else's table and pouring it into my glass, I drank half of it in one big gulp and made my way to the bar. I know, I know, Franki was smart to make everyone swear off eating or drinking until it was determined what poisoned Amber. But this bottle had been on that table all night, and I was willing to take a chance, considering who I'd be interviewing.

Chelsea saw me coming and grimaced. She got up and walked over to where Charlene was sitting. Her surly sister looked up from her book, scowled, and went back to reading, until I pulled out a chair and joined them.

"Hey, guys!" I said brightly. "Fun party! Okay, so the bride-to-be is missing and her fiancé's ex is dead, but other than that, not too shabby." I looked around a room that seemed to be begging someone to commit arson to put it out of its misery. "Okay, so pretty shabby. But hey! We're all friends now, which is a total win."

"This is your fault!" Chelsea pointed a finger at me.

I gasped in mock surprise. "I don't see how."

Chelsea narrowed her eyes. "*You* invited that stupid Amber. And then *you* didn't throw her out like I told you to. Now she's dead and the party is ruined!"

Charlene frowned as she looked around. "She's kind of right, Chels. I never really noticed what a dump this was. Why did you pick this place?"

"I didn't invite Amber," I said before her sister could respond. "She wasn't on the list you sent. Which makes me wonder who *did* invite her?"

Chelsea's eyes bulged. "*I* didn't invite her! I couldn't stand that bimbo! Charlie dumped her, and she was always coming around, trying to get back together with him! As if someone like her is good enough for my brother!"

With an *I-don't-buy-it* expression I usually reserved for waterboarding Russians, I turned my attention to Charlene.

"I didn't invite her either," she snorted derisively. "I don't like her *or* Babette. I've been trying to get Charlie to raise his standards."

"Right." I theorized. "Then Charlie invited her."

The smug looks on the sisters' faces froze.

I continued. "If neither one of you invited her, and I doubt that the agent, the hand model, that weird party crasher, Candace, or the grocery store manager did, that leaves Charlie." I paused a bit before going on. "Which begs the question, why would Babette's fiancé invite his ex-girlfriend to her bachelorette party?"

"It couldn't have been Charlie." Chelsea folded her arms. "He would never…" Her voice trailed off, telling me she wasn't entirely confident that Charlie hadn't invited Amber.

I shook my head. "And it means that Charlie is a complete jerk, and that's what I'm going to tell his fiancée when she gets here." I sat back and drained my glass of wine while maintaining eye contact—which really works better when the glass is full, but I think I pulled it off.

"Charlie is a gentleman." Chelsea's voice dripped with fury. Even if she wasn't totally convinced of his innocence, she doubled down. "He would never do something so underhanded and sneaky."

Charlene nodded, but I thought I saw doubt in her angry eyes. It seemed to me she was hiding something. But what? Suspicions about Charlie? Or her sister Chelsea? Even though she insisted the family was innocent, someone wasn't telling me the truth. I just didn't know if they were lying about how Amber came to be here or who killed her.

"Amber might've found out about the party somehow," Chelsea said with a little less rage. "Maybe she knows Mo and he told her, and she crashed the party in a bid to win Charlie back." She hesitated before changing her mind. "But I don't think that's what happened. You blew it. I told you not to invite her!"

This again? "You never told me anything about her. She wasn't on the list you sent and, aside from Babette, I didn't know anyone else connected to invite before this evening. I didn't even know Amber existed." I leaned forward. "But you two did."

Neither sister said anything, which was their only real defense.

I pressed them. "And I think you invited her to get Babette to call off the wedding. Do you deny that?"

A vein popped out on Chelsea's neck and began to throb. "We didn't invite Amber! We hate her!"

"Do you hate her enough to kill her?" I said quickly.

Chelsea's mouth dropped open. "What? No!"

"I mean," I went on, "if some bimbo crashed *my* brother's party in order to get him to break up with his fiancée, I might think of taking her out back and teaching her a lesson."

The truth is, I don't have a brother. I'm an only child. But I meant what I said. I'd defend my mythical brother from his equally mythical ex. It's a matter of nonexistent sibling loyalty.

"You don't have to have invited her to kill her," I continued. "In fact, her crashing the party just gives you two another motive to want her dead."

My cell phone buzzed one time in my pocket, but I ignored it. It was probably from home, and I didn't want to hear from Hilly or Betty or about my burned garage.

"Charlie is a saint," Charlene said finally. "He's too nice to kick Amber out, even if she is awful."

"Ah. So *he* killed her."

"No! You're doing this wrong!" Charlene sputtered.

I spread my hands out. "Doing what wrong?"

"This…this…thing!" For someone who read the classics, she sure was having trouble trying to decide what to say. Melville never ran out of things to say. Which was probably why I've never gotten all the way through *Moby Dick*.

"What are you talking about?" I asked.

Charlene opened her mouth and then closed it. Apparently she didn't know what she was talking about either.

The cell buzzed once again. I continued to ignore it.

Chelsea barked, "Charlie was out of Amber's league, and she knew it! She wanted to climb the social ladder using him to get there."

"I see." I nodded. "You're jet-setting socialites, and Amber was having ideas above her station."

I wasn't a big fan of stuff like that. Iowans came from pioneer stock. Those who settled in my fair state didn't have time to throw debutante balls or gala fundraisers. They were too busy keeping their children alive and the crops from dying…usually at the same time.

But that didn't matter, because I was pretty sure Chelsea, Charlene, and Charlie weren't the blue bloods that Chelsea insisted they were. There were lots of reasons, but the biggest one was that nobody with any amount of social grace would name a baby Charlene, with a hard *Ch*.

"Yes." Chelsea sniffed. "If you must know, my family belongs to a country club, and we have Merry Maids clean our houses once a week."

"And I'm well-educated," Charlene added.

Chelsea stared at her sister. "So am I. We all are."

"Please! You took an online course in business for a certificate from the Buffalo Business Institute," Charlene snapped. "*I* went to Mount Holyoke!"

"Yes," Chelsea said meanly. "For one semester before you quit!"

Charlene turned red. "It counts! Besides, it took you years to get your pharmaceutical degree and, when you did, it was from an online, for-profit college in Venezuela that's currently being investigated for fraud!"

We were getting off track. I needed something from them to help me and the others determine if these two were suspects. So far, all I knew was that they hadn't invited Amber, hated her guts, and considered themselves to be some sort of Niagara Falls royalty.

"All right." I held up my hands. "If you didn't kill Amber, who do you think did?"

"You did it!" Chelsea said. "You're ex-CIA!"

I shook my head. "Again, I didn't know Amber even *existed* until she dropped dead in front of me tonight."

"That pregnant woman went into the bathroom with her!" Charlene snapped.

"There are four of us here who have never met any of you, had never met Charlie, and didn't know Amber was even a thing," I said levelly. "Valentine, Franki, Kate, and I are in the clear as far as I'm concerned." Look at me, defending my new friends!

My cell buzzed once with another text. Something was up, and I'd need to deal with that soon.

"She went in the bathroom with her," Charlene scowled. "And isn't she from San Francisco? Didn't Amber die while eating Ghirardelli chocolates?"

She had a point. But I didn't think Kate killed Amber. First of all, she was too smart to give the victim poisoned chocolates with symbols from her hometown. Secondly, the woman was, like, seriously pregnant.

Although, I shouldn't count that in her favor. I once knew a Yemeni assassin who only hunted her targets in the third trimester of her many pregnancies. She said it was because of rage brought on by hormones, but I think she was just bored and needed something to do.

When she wasn't pregnant, Bibi was actually very sweet. She once gave me a pillow on which she'd needlepointed *DEATH TO AMERICAN SCUM* in pretty script with little hearts and flowers. I still have it in a box. In the garage that I may or may not have anymore.

Chelsea and Charlene were suspects, I decided. They could've worked together, maybe even with Charlie, but I wasn't sure of that. What I did know was that these two women were angry about nearly everything, were keeping things from me, and were certainly capable of murder. They didn't like Amber, and either they invited her to kill her, or when Amber crashed the party to win Charlie back, they decided to remove this low-class interloper from his life.

My cell buzzed longer, indicating that this time it was a call.

"I have to take this," I said as I got up from the table and stepped away.

"Mrs. Ferguson?" A nervous male voice said as he uttered my married name. I'm called Wrath so much I sometimes forget I have a different last name now. "This is your insurance agent."

I could picture the guy, but his name eluded me. "Oh. Hi. What's your name again?"

There was a brief moment of silence. "I'd rather not tell you if you don't mind. Also, I'm moving to…somewhere else. Therefore, I won't be your agent anymore after the end of the month."

What a weird thing to call about on a weekend night. "Is that why you called? I'm kind of in the middle of something."

A female voice on the other end said something I couldn't quite make out.

Insurance Guy continued. "Anyway, I'm going to check out the damage on your home tomorrow."

This was followed by more female mumbling in the background.

"I'm sorry, I mean I'll check it out right away." His voice squeaked a little.

I sighed. That sounded bad. I'd kind of hoped Hilly had been pranking me with the garage thing. In any event, the man sounded very stressed out. "Is everything all right…um…Anonymous Insurance Guy?"

His voice quavered as if he was terrified. "Yes. In fact, I don't need to see the property. We'll pay the whole thing. You don't even need to pay the deductible."

My heart sank. I guess the embroidered pillow from the Yemeni assassin was toast. I wondered if that was covered as a one-of-a-kind art piece.

Then I remembered what he'd just said. "You're going to pay for all the damage without seeing it?"

"Of course!" he said quickly. "Miss Vinton explained it all. Don't worry about a thing."

Great. Hilly was intimidating him. That was all I needed. Then again, she was getting results.

"Who's taking your place?" I asked. "Who'll be my new insurance agent?"

"I have no idea, but it won't be me." His voice was grim. "You could do me a favor, though. Will you talk to Miss Vinton and tell her everything is all right? I don't like the way she's holding that hammer…"

I was right. "Sure, put her on."

"Hi, Merry! You really got a good deal! I wish *my* insurance agent were as eager to help. He wouldn't reimburse me for my

Lexus just because someone threw themselves in front of it and then the blood wouldn't come off the bumper."

That brought me up short. "You have a Lexus?"

"Not anymore," Hilly said. "I'm in the market. I'll need something with a red paint job."

"Okay. But please let Insurance Guy go. He has work to do."

Hilly agreed and hung up before I realized I didn't ask her how bad the damage was. Oh, well. Complete coverage and no deductible! That felt like a win.

I turned back to the table to find the sisters gone. Great. And I was just about to threaten to break out the waterboarding.

# BABETTE

## LESLIE LANGTRY

*T*he trip to the police station was the absolute *worst*—
and not just because they practically had to wedge me
into the backseat with a shoehorn. How did this happen? I didn't
*do* anything! Yes, I look like a hot dog with a wire coming out of
it, but how many terrorists wear food costumes before blowing
themselves up? There's no dignity in that. I knew firsthand
because getting arrested while wearing this suit had destroyed
whatever was left of mine.

This was the last straw! I wasn't going to get bossed into
portraying talking junk food ever again. Acting work or no
acting work—this was not worth it. Why can't my agent find me
a part in a commercial where I play a doctor with luxurious
blonde hair, or a concert pianist dripping in expensive jewelry, or
a nun with a brilliant flair for accessorizing? I could do any and
all of those, *and* it would have the added bonus of being able to fit
into a car.

Sitting in the back of the police cruiser with both hands
cuffed in front of me gave me a lot of perspective, which was an
improvement over my fog of confusion as they arrested me.

Holy cow! I'm not only missing my party but I'm about to be

booked for something I didn't do! At least, I *think* I didn't do anything. I know I'm not a terrorist. And soon they'll find that out.

All I wanted was to hit the pawnshop and pick up my grandmother's bracelet, go to my party, and drink myself silly with my friends. I'd been so excited that I was finally getting Valentine, Kate, Merry, and Franki together. Even though they were very different, I just knew they'd like each other. And with me, we'd be the Fabsome Five! Don't you love it? I made up *fabsome* all by myself! I made a mental note to explore printing that on pink T-shirts.

The squad car parked in front of the station, and the officer who'd been driving got out and opened my door. Unfortunately, the extra foot of hot dog on top of my head had been wedged firmly against the roof of the car.

The policeman reached inside and yanked the rounded end downward, which unfortunately brought my head down until the wiener top was stopped by the plexiglass in between the bench seats, where its rigidity pinned me against my seat.

"This is Robins," I heard the cop say into his radio. "I need assistance. Can someone bring the jaws of life?"

Part of me was secretly thrilled to destroy this ridiculous costume, but the other part knew I'd be in deep trouble if I did.

"Hold on!" I shouted as I struggled, turned to the left, and finally popped myself out of the car.

"Cancel that order," Officer Robins said. "Ma'am, you'll have to come with me."

I was led into the building and taken to a room where they chained my cuffed hands to a table. The walls were gray, the ceiling was gray, the floor was gray, and so were the table and chairs. Good grief, this place badly needed a makeover! If they asked me, I'd say go with a pale watercolor green to promote a soothing atmosphere. Wasn't that what they wanted? Calm convicts? It made sense to me.

Before I could even attempt to get comfortable, two women police officers came in.

"I'm Officer Jones," the tall redhead said before pointing to a brunette of average height. "That's Officer Saunders."

"Hello!" I tried to wave, but my wrist was pinned to the table. "I'm Babette Lang." I thought for a second. "I don't always wear a wiener costume," I added.

Jones and Saunders unchained me and began to frisk the wiener, which I think made us all uncomfortable. I mentally cursed my boss and agent. They were going to hear from Babette Lang when this was over.

"We're going to have to impound the hot dog," Officer Jones said. "What are you wearing underneath?"

"Not much," I admitted.

Officer Saunders looked me over and then left, returning momentarily with a pair of light gray scrubs. It took a while, but eventually, with help from the policewomen, I got out of the hot dog and into the scrubs. The scrubs, while being much more comfortable than the costume, weren't exactly flattering. What was it with gray in this place? Why not try something else, like pastel pink or cornflower blue? I look great in those two colors.

I stretched my arms to the ceiling and bent over to touch my toes. Who knew clothes this ugly could feel so amazing?

"I'll have to cuff you again," Saunders said apologetically.

That was disappointing. "Okay." I held out my hands.

The two women exchanged a glance before Jones said, "Looks like the so-called bomb was just a loose wire in her costume. I don't think we need to cuff her."

Saunders rolled her eyes. "Leave it to a bunch of men to think a woman in a hot dog suit is a terrorist." She patted my arm. "Sit down, please." And then they left the room.

I slumped in the chair. At least it sounded like the terrorist charge would be thrown out. And while I certainly didn't want to get back into that costume again, I was really getting worried about the party.

My friends had gone to a lot of work for me to be a no-show. And what about Charlie? He must be worried sick. Hopefully, I'd get my one phone call, and I could call him.

Wait. Was Charlie really the best option? I loved him and all that, but when he got worried, he started to panic. I needed someone with a cool head, which meant one of my four friends. They would be the most reliable.

I could call Kate, but the woman was super-pregnant, and the last thing she needed in her condition was to come down to the station. Merry was a possibility. She was ex-CIA, which seemed like a plus, and had lots of experience with terrorists, which now that I thought about it might be more detrimental to my defense as an *accused* terrorist.

That left Franki and Valentine. Franki was a cool customer and as a private eye would be helpful. Then again, Valentine could come down and charm the whole department into letting me go.

Oh wait…I lost my phone to the Falls, and I had no idea what their numbers were. In fact, I wasn't even sure I knew Charlie's number. Nope. I didn't. Dang. Who memorizes phone numbers these days?

I was wondering how I could get hold of people without knowing their phone numbers when two identical men in black suits walked in and closed the door. They both wore earpieces connected to a wire that ran down their necks into their collars, and they both wore the same black mirrored sunglasses. Someone should really explain accessorizing to them.

"I'm Agent Summer, and this is Agent Winter. We're with the Federal Bureau of Investigation." He glanced at my hands on the table and jumped back with a look of horror on his face. "Why isn't she chained?"

"Code RED!" Agent Winter shouted and ran out the door while Summer pulled his gun on me.

"You stay right there and leave your hands on the table!" He looked seriously upset, so I did what he asked.

Winter came back in with handcuffs, which he used to chain my wrists to the table. Then he put manacles on my ankles and fastened them to an iron ring on the floor. What was happening? Officers Jones and Saunders said *they* didn't think I was a terrorist!

"Leave it to a couple of women to underestimate their opponent and leave her unrestrained," Winter said to Summer, who nodded.

"Um, I'm really not all that dangerous," I began.

Summer slapped his hand on the table, and I jumped. "Tell it to the Marines, sister!"

Why would I tell *it*, whatever *it* was, to the Marines? What did that mean?

"Nice one." Winter snickered before waving his finger at me. "You're in big trouble in little China, lady!"

"Look," I said carefully. "I'm just an actress who dressed as a hot dog to hand out wiener samples at the Falls…"

Winter immediately clapped a hand to his earpiece. "Someone needs to get out to the Falls! She's been handing out food that may be poisoned! Prepare for mass casualties!"

"Mass casualties?" I squeaked. "Poison?" The worst that could happen was ptomaine, and while I wouldn't put it past that cheapskate boss of mine to serve up bad meat, it certainly wouldn't have been intentional.

"Look…" Summer smiled in a way that was more deranged than reassuring. "We get it. Your people have been oppressed. We've got it coming. Blah, blah, blah." He gave a furtive nod to Winter. "Just give us what we need, and we'll cut a deal."

I finally found my voice. "I'm telling you the truth! I'm no terrorist!"

Winter took a turn slamming his hand on the table. "That's exactly what a terrorist would say!"

I changed my mind. Maybe I did need Merry.

"Listen," I tried to push back. "Call my boss, Stanley, at Higgly Piggly. He'll tell you!"

Summer put his hand up to his ear and repeated what I'd just said. "Sounds like the terrorist cell operates using a grocery store as a front to sell weapons and make bombs."

"No," I said. "It just sells groceries."

"Who are you with? The Taliban? Hamas? FARC? Boko Haram? Monkey Vagina?"

"Monkey what?" I asked. "There's a terrorist group called that?"

Winter nodded. "It's a group from Uzbekistan that speaks a very obscure dialect, and that's the best translation we could work out."

Summer raised his hand. "I, for one, think it's Monkey *Fist*, but these guys won't listen to me."

Winter looked over his shoulder. "Would you stop undermining me in front of the terrorist?"

"I'm not a terrorist!" I said a bit more forcefully.

Summer scowled. "I wasn't undermining you in front of the terrorist. I just think that's the right translation, and in fact, Monkey Fist sounds scarier. Just saying."

Winter glared at me.

"I agree with Summer," I said meekly. I probably shouldn't have, but he was right. "Monkey Fist is way better."

The disgruntled Fed pointed at me, then looked at his partner. "See? Now you've got the terrorist twisting my words and trying to confuse me!"

"I kind of think you're doing that to yourself," Summer admonished. "Remember what your therapist told you? You have to stop thinking everyone is against you."

"I think your therapist is right," I added. Maybe I could get

Summer on my side. I batted my eyelash extensions for good measure.

Winter gave me a nod. "She's Monkey Vagina all right. Notice how she plays us against each other in order to confuse us?"

"You may be right." Summer narrowed his eyes at me. "We haven't had any terrorism in this district, but it was only a matter of time before someone put a hot dog costume over a suicide vest."

"Look," I summoned my inner strength. "I'm not a terrorist. And I think I want a lawyer." My voice grew sterner. "I'm late for my own bachelorette party at the Park Avenue Hotel. My fiancé must be worried he hasn't heard from me, and my friends must be going crazy. I'm not going to talk to you any more without a lawyer."

I sat back in my chair, trying to look tough, even though I was screaming inside.

Summer and Winter exchanged glances.

Summer leaned forward. "Did you say you're supposed to be at a party at the Park Avenue?"

I nodded, but true to my word, did not speak.

Without saying anything, both men walked out of the gray room. It gave me a small amount of hope. Surely they understood that no terrorist would be worried about missing her bachelorette party.

Terrorists didn't think about parties and decorations and cake. At least, I didn't *think* they cared about those things. I felt myself relaxing for the first time since I put on that dumb suit. At any moment, those smart women cops would come in and let me go. Hopefully, they wouldn't make me change back into the wiener costume.

I wasn't totally surprised when that was what happened. Officers Saunders and Jones came in and unchained me. I could've hugged them both.

"Is there anything you want after that fiasco?" Jones asked.

"I could *murder* for a cup of coffee!" I said.

The two officers seemed uncomfortable with my statement, but Jones went out and brought back a steaming mug.

"Thank you!" I batted my eyelash extensions at them. It couldn't hurt, right? I mean, you never know.

"Don't thank us yet," Saunders said.

Huh? "Why not?"

A short, pudgy, middle-aged man entered the room, carrying a file folder and wearing a cheap suit and an air of near-constant exhaustion.

"Miss Lang. I'm Detective Bourbon." He slapped the folder onto the table. "I'm happy to say that the Feds have decided you're not a member of Monkey, uh, whatever."

Jones and Saunders rolled their eyes.

The detective squinted at his notes. "That's what it says, all right." He sighed. "Anyway, that, combined with the fact that the suit had no explosives wired inside, puts you in the clear."

"Yay!" I sprang out of the chair and clapped my hands. "Can I go? And can I keep these scrubs? I'll pay for them, I swear."

"Sit down, please," Detective Bourbon said in an authoritarian tone that seemed to come from nowhere.

I sat.

"Like I said, we no longer believe you're a terrorist. But we do have another issue that maybe you can clear up."

"Um, okay." I bit my lower lip and looked at Officers Jones and Saunders. They shook their heads. That didn't seem like a good sign.

Bourbon looked me in the eye. "The party you mentioned is currently under investigation."

Uh-oh. "Look," I said quickly. "Merry isn't a terrorist. She's ex-CIA. I know that can seem a little scary, but she's really nice and..."

Bourbon shook his head. "It isn't that, although I will make a note of it. The reason for the current investigation is that one of your guests has been murdered."

"What?" My hands flew up to my chest.

"And we'd like to talk to you about that." He settled into a chair, and it creaked beneath him.

"Murder?" I asked. "That's impossible! There was going to be cake, and fun cocktails, and my friends, but no murder!"

"Are you saying you know nothing about it?" Bourbon asked.

I shook my head. "I haven't even made it to the party yet! Please tell me it wasn't one of my friends—Valentine, Merry, Kate, or Franki!" I remembered something. "Or my fiancé, Charlie, who technically isn't supposed to be there, but knowing Charlie…"

"No, it wasn't anyone by those names." Bourbon relaxed visibly.

"Was it Zelda or Chelsea or Charlene?" I made sure to pronounce Charlene with a hard *Ch*. That woman hated me, and she hated any mispronunciation of her name.

The detective looked at his notes. "No, it wasn't any of them."

"Then who was it? I can't think of anyone else." I began to chew on my lip again. "Maybe you have the wrong party?"

Detective Bourbon shook his head. "It wasn't anyone you named. Can you think of someone else who might be there?"

I shook my head.

He waited a moment before asking, "Do you know a woman named Amber O'Grady?"

My mouth dropped open, and my stomach dropped. "What was Amber doing at my party?"

# FRANKI

## TRACI ANDRIGHETTI

*Z*elda elbowed my side with such force that my head jerked and I nearly fell from my barstool. "Get a load o' that medical examiner, Frenchie." She cackled. "The guy looks like he's at death's door."

*Said the old woman who just put in her teeth, pushed up her wig, and couldn't remember my name.* "Shh." I rubbed my now aching neck. "I'm waiting to hear what he says to the detective about Amber."

"What for? We all know the Pregasaurus killed that bimbo."

Even though Kate's belly was the size of a dinosaur egg, I glared for good measure. "She'll kill *you* if you don't watch out. And you're awfully quick to point the finger. Did *you* have a motive to kill Amber?"

Her lined lids lowered. "Who are you to ask me that?"

"A PI. This is how we solve cases."

"Well, you can forget that baloney commercial. You and I are through." Zelda pulled out her teeth and tossed them into her bag.

*That was one way to end a conversation—and a cold cuts career.*

The medical examiner rose on seventy-something-year-old

legs with the help of the detective, who was at least sixty himself, and flipped long, wispy bangs onto his bald head. "I'll have to run a tox panel and examine her stomach contents, but this has all the markers of opioid poisoning."

*The same thing the paramedics told Merry.*

The detective rubbed a scar on his chin as he studied the chocolate residue on Amber's blue lips. "Any track marks or bruises?"

"Didn't see any, not even under the nails."

"Either she took the drugs herself, or someone slipped them into her drink...or those chocolates." His hawk eye landed on the Ghirardelli box that the forensic team was bagging for the lab. "Odd the bachelorette is MIA."

*My thoughts exactly. But what was he implying? That Babette could be dead? Or that she was the killer?*

"Call me after the autopsy, Doc." The detective turned and approached Chelsea, whose perfectly pressed suit was beginning to wrinkle.

I slid off my barstool and joined Valentine and Kate at a table. "Has anyone heard from Babette?"

Valentine shook her head. "Not a word, and we've been trying to reach her."

I didn't want to mention my fear that Babette might have met the same fate as Amber. Instead, I glanced at Merry, who was on her phone in a corner. "Any chance she's talking to the bachelorette?"

"No." Kate propped her feet on a chair. "It's some insurance guy."

*She's probably taking out a last-minute policy because of this killer party.*

Merry hung up, and I waved her over. She was en route to our table when the detective raised his hand. "Ms. Wrath," he called in an I'm-really-ready-to-retire tone, "I need a word."

Kate's eyes grew as big as her dinosaur egg. "What does he want with Merry?"

Valentine opened her compact and spied the detective in the reflection of her mirror. "It could be because she's ex-CIA."

"Whoa. I had no idea." But it explained a lot—the zip ties, the drug knowledge, and the chutzpah to take on a Girl Scout troop.

Kate crossed her arms. "I'll bet it's because of Chelsea and Charlene. To take the suspicion off them and their awful brother, they accused Merry of inviting Amber to the party."

Valentine shook her head. "The detective won't fall for that. Amber's not on the invitation list, and Merry had never heard of her before today. None of us had."

I surveyed the party guests. "Then who *did* invite Amber?"

Valentine snapped the compact shut. "Either she heard about the party somehow and decided to crash it, or Charlie invited her."

Rock could have told Amber that he was working the shindig, but I doubted it. Her so-called hand-holding fetish had really weirded him out. "Charlie seems like a lowlife, but is he so lowdown that he'd invite his ex to his future bride's bachelorette party?"

Kate harrumphed. "When I asked him how Amber had gotten the chocolates after he took them to Babette's room, he accused Babette of sneaking back to the hotel to kill her."

I sidelined the unanswerable *What does Babette see in that bum?* in favor of "Why would he say such a despicable thing?"

"He claims Babette hated Amber."

"That's ridiculous. And how would Babette kill Amber when she's not even here?"

Valentine leaned forward. "When Kate and I went into Babette's room, we found Fentanyl in her pharma suitcase."

My head recoiled. Between Zelda's elbow whack and the opioid stash, I was going to get whiplash. "Was it pills?"

"A vial of liquid. Why?"

"Amber could've taken the pills, but she would've had to inject the liquid, and the medical examiner said she didn't have any needle marks. I guess Rock could've poured it in her drink. He had a one-night stand with Amber while she was dating Charlie."

Valentine eyed the gloved bartender. "I don't *think* he's left the bar since we got here, but I can't account for where he was when Kate and I were in Babette's room, which doesn't help since that was *after* Amber died."

Kate caught Valentine's gaze. "What about Charlene?"

"What about her?" I held up my hands. "I mean, besides her desperate need of an anger management class."

Valentine pursed her frosted lips. "I saw her leave the room, and she's using a bookmark with *Fentanyl* scribbled on it."

I leaned back in my chair. "She could be taking it for pain—or to help her get through *Moby Dick*. But we need to tell the detective."

"If we tell him about the bookmark," Kate said between chewing her thumbnail, "then we'll have to tell him about the Fentanyl in Babette's suitcase."

"Don't worry." I patted her back. "The pharmaceutical company will vouch for her having the drug. And she's been at the Falls passing out wieners, so she has an alibi."

Valentine tugged at a glittery hoop earring like she was considering something. "I just hope none of her Fentanyl samples are missing. That reminds me, Franki, Babette's suitcase is almost identical to yours, which might be why Charlie overreacted when he saw it behind the bar."

I ran my hand across my chin while I processed the news. "Okay, but why did he try to open it when I'd told him earlier that it was mine?"

"He's so drunk, he probably forgot."

*Or he had a sinister motive.*

Kate rubbed her belly. "What if the detective believes Charlie?

Babette could be arrested for murder at her own bachelorette party."

I stood and grabbed my hobo bag. "We'll have to make sure that doesn't happen. What's her room number?"

Valentine's eyes widened. "It's 418. What do you have planned?"

"I need to check those Fentanyl vials."

She glanced behind her at the detective. "I have a key card, but it doesn't work."

My look was pointed. "You might want to get rid of that, or you could end up a suspect."

Kate touched my forearm. "You could be a suspect too if the detective catches you, or even go to jail."

"Trust me, if this hotel is any indication of the condition of the jail, I'd throw myself over the Falls before I'd let myself be locked up in this town. As far as the detective is concerned, I'm in the ladies' room." I waited until his back was to me, then I slipped into the hallway. Something about Charlie rifling through my suitcase didn't feel right. *Was he looking for something to steal? Or was Valentine right about him forgetting the suitcase was mine?* If the latter was true, he was looking for drugs. *But were they for him? Or for someone else?*

Mo was behind the reception counter watching the credits to *Weekend at Bernie's*. His zip ties had been replaced with handcuffs, which set off a police siren in my head. "What's going on, Mo? Did you kill Amber?"

"Slow down there, Francy. That ain't my kind of crime."

*What was it with people in Niagara Falls and my name?* "It's *Franki*, and something landed you in those handcuffs."

"Yeah, a warrant for lifting a guy's wallet."

The pickpocket revelation put a new spin on his affection for Hot Pockets.

He jerked his head to flip what was left of his bangs. "Detective van der Donk and I go way back, to Niagara Street Elementary."

I'd have to process that surname later. "Maybe you should learn a lesson from him about living on the straight and narrow since you two went to school together."

"That ain't what I meant. Don's got ten years on me. Been locking me up since I was a kid."

*Don? Don van der Donk?*

Mo turned sideways, used his fingers to slide the remote between his hands, and aimed it behind his back at the television. He was remarkably adept at functioning with his hands cuffed, which underscored his lengthy arrest history.

My cell rang. *My parents' number. Nope.* I dropped the phone into my bag. "Listen, Mo, I need your help."

The hotel phone began to ring.

"Hold that request." Mo used his mouth to knock the receiver to the counter and pressed his ear to it. "Park Avenue Hotel. I'm tied up at the moment. Can you call back?" He eyed my chest and not because his head was on the counter. "Sure is." He paused. "I feel ya. Kids are hard. Got a few myself."

*Great. A personal call.*

"When they're small, you love 'em, feed 'em, let 'em steal your beer and cigarettes. Then they grow up and go out in the world, and all's you can do is hope for the best."

His kids' futures didn't sound too promising. But, come to think of it, I'd stolen my dad's beer. *What did that say about how I'd turned out?* I'd have to ponder that along with the name Don van der Donk.

I leaned on the counter. A key card in an envelope marked room 418 lay on the workspace below. *What was* that *doing out?*

Mo switched to his other ear, turning toward the TV, and I slid the key card from the envelope and took the elevator to the fourth floor, which was deserted. We were probably the only fools in the hotel.

I inserted the key card into the slot and entered Babette's room. The suitcase was beneath the window, and I would've sworn it was mine. Using a tissue from the nightstand, I flipped open the latches and rummaged through the pill bottles until I found four Fentanyl vials. One had half the liquid of the others.

"*Mannaggia,*" I said, cursing at the bottle in Italian. The missing Fentanyl had to be the murder weapon.

Babette, Charlie, Kate, Valentine, and I had been in the room. *But who else?* Since the key card was on the reception counter, anyone could have come in.

With a heavy sigh, I looked around for any evidence. On the dresser was a monthly magazine called *Things to Do in Niagara Falls*, and beneath it the room service menu. I flipped it open. Hot Pockets. Go figure. Mo was dining on the hotel's dime. *But had he committed a harder crime than petty theft?*

I opened the nightstand drawer. *The Holy Bible.* God knows the guests at this hellhole needed it. Pen beside the phone—but no pad of paper with the hotel letterhead. All hotels have that, even dumps like this one. I crouched to check under the bed. To avoid touching the carpet, I made like Mo and put my hands behind my back. Nothing except for an inch of dust bunnies.

And then I saw it.

A pad had fallen between the nightstand and the bed. I fished it out and ran the pen over the top page. Two words appeared. "*Niagara Collateral.* What's that?"

Shoving the pad into my bag, I left the room and returned to the reception desk. Mo was still on the phone with his face glued to the TV.

I slid the key card back into the envelope and caught the title of the movie—*Weekend at Bernie's II.* I added Mo to my suspect list. The guy had a thing for movies about people partying with a corpse, which was a little too similar to what was happening at the hotel.

"Fuggedabout it." Mo chuckled, and his gray skin turned

almost beige. "Call anytime you need to vent, you hear?" He straightened and gave me a death stare. "It's your mother, and speaking of lessons, you could learn a lot from her."

*Mo and my mom commiserating on child-rearing? No wonder I'd ended up in a sleazy hotel with a pickpocket receptionist and a homicidal maniac.*

He bent to pick up the receiver with his lips, and I shoved his shoulder. "I'll get it with my hand, thank you."

Rather than reuse the tissue from Babette's room—since one use was all the cheap things could handle—I pulled a fresh one from a box on the counter and picked up the phone. "What's up, Mom?"

"I just had a lovely conversation with the reception clerk. That man's a saint."

*Funny, because his handcuffs said sinner.*

"Anyway, your nonna and I were chatting, and we think it would be fun if you have an out-of-town bachelorette party like, say, in Houston at our house."

I knew it would be bad if my family found out where I was. "You know that Bradley and I aren't getting married until next year."

"There's no law against planning ahead, Francesca."

"She's-a right, Franki," Nonna chimed in from the other line. "Remember the old-a proverb, 'He who sleep-a don't catch-a the fish—or the husband.'"

*Who could forget the Italian version of "the early bird catches the worm—and a husband"?* "I'm not going to plan my bachelorette party while I'm at someone else's."

"What better time, dear? You can get ideas."

*About everything* not *to do for a party.* "I've got to run. I'm working."

"Francesca Lucia Amato," she shouted in her you're-grounded voice, "you know better than to lie to your mother."

Mo must've heard her because he gave me a don't-talk-to-your-mother-that-way look, to which I replied with a keep-looking-at-me-like-that-and-I'll-clock-you-with-this-phone look. I had enough on my party plate without being co-parented by a Hot-Pockets-gobbling pickpocket. "It's the truth, Mom. A guest died, and it was foul play."

She gasped. "Is that why the groom was screaming when I called earlier?"

"Yeah, he used to date her."

"*Madonna mia!*" Nonna wailed. "How old-a is-a this-a woman?"

I glanced toward the hallway to check for the detective. "Late twenties, maybe?"

"You mark-a my words-a, that-a bachelorette did it!"

"Nonna, why would you accuse Babette of something so awful?"

"Because-a the woman who die has got-a young-a eggs."

"Oh, thank heavens!" My mother breathed. "That means you're safe, Francesca."

I handed the phone to Mo's mouth. He took one look at my face and didn't give me any grief. His lips gripped the receiver and hung it up.

"Here's the deal," I said, giving Mo a hard stare. "After I checked in, I saw Amber swapping saliva with a guy in the elevator, and you're going to tell me who it was."

His shifty eyes shifted. "You didn't hear this from me, but it was that bachelor, Charlie."

*I knew it.*

"I seen him around town in the clubs. That lucky schmuck gets all the babes. But if he'd gotten in that elevator five minutes earlier, he would've lost the bachelorette."

"'Lost' in what sense?"

"As in, she would've called off the wedding. He just missed his bride-to-be."

I gripped the counter. "Babette was here?"

"That's what I'm trying to tell you. She came back right before Charlie went upstairs with Amber, but she was in and out so fast that I didn't have a chance to hit her up for any wiener samples." He flashed teeth still flecked with mozzarella. "Pop a couple of dogs in a Hot Pocket, and that's good eats."

I blinked, speechless, and not because of his Babette revelation. "Is that her key card on the counter?"

His head bobbed. "Yeah. I had to make her a new one after she lost the first one. She says she left it on the counter, but it ain't here."

*Because Valentine borrowed it.*

"I haven't put this one away on account o' the handcuffs."

And yet, he'd managed to operate the remote control and the phone. "Why would she come back during the party and not tell her guests?"

He rolled his shoulders. "Said she had to take care of something to secure her future."

*Her future? With Charlie?* I swallowed and tried not to think of the cheese in Mo's teeth. *Was my nonna right?*

*Did Babette kill Amber?*

# VALENTINE

## ARLENE MCFARLANE

*M*erry shifted her gaze to Kate and me after talking to Detective van der Donk—who I concluded was nowhere near as hot and sexy as Romero. Okay, I reasoned, not every detective had movie-star looks, a hard-ass swagger, and moves that weren't covered in a police handbook.

I sighed, and my heart gave a heavy thud. It'd been less than twenty-four hours since Romero had practiced some of those moves on me. Surely I wouldn't combust before experiencing another night of steamy passion. Right. Tell that to someone who'd never been kissed by the six-foot, hot-blooded Italian.

Thank heavens Franki sauntered into the room before I forgot why I was here. After all, I had more dire things to think about at the moment than my love life.

I looked from Franki to Merry as they merged and headed our way. My pulse was pounding so fast and I was so full of questions, I didn't know where to begin.

I was debating who to probe first, and before I reached a decision, Candace hustled up to us, red spikes click-clacking to an abrupt halt on the patch of floor by the bar. The look on her face said she was not happy. "What a waste of time, flying in for *this*.

I've been to funerals that were more fun. At least there was a body."

We cast our eyes down to the spot where Amber had just been removed, Candace's choice of words likely not fazing her. The others fell silent and backed away, wisely staying out of the crossfire between my nemesis and me.

"What the hell happened to Babette, anyway? She should've been here hours ago."

I pushed down a hard swallow at the turn of events, then squared my shoulders and met Candace's stare. "Since you were such close buddies in Drama Club, why don't you call her and ask where she is?"

"Very *funny*. Maybe we haven't been in touch for a long time. That doesn't mean she wouldn't be happy to see me."

"Happy as in jumping for joy? Or as in *She was happy to have a sedative before her colonoscopy?*"

Her eyes turned to slits, her baby blues barely visible. "You're a barrel of laughs, Valentine. You're as bad as all the other losers here. That boss of Babette's, for one, seems to have had it in for her. I wouldn't be surprised if he'd bumped her off and dumped her body in the Falls. That sloppy jacket he's wearing is full of water spots, and he's got yellow gunk on his sleeves. He also smells like he had a mustard bath."

Water spots? Mustard stains? How'd I miss that? Of course, I hadn't been sitting next to him like Candace had, watching his arm swing up and down as he popped cream puffs into his mouth.

"And that grim reaper, Charlene. If *she* isn't the life of the party! I couldn't *wait* to get away from her and her dreary book. Who reads about Jonah and the whale at a bachelorette party, anyway?"

Leave it to Candace to confuse a biblical prophet for Captain Ahab.

"Would you believe she even has a bookmark with *Fentanyl*

written on it? When I asked why, she said, 'You never know when you might need the name of a lethal drug.'"

Candace tugged her red tube top up with her red dagger fingernails. "You should've seen the wicked grin on her face when she said it, too."

I kept a straight face. In all honesty, I wasn't sure Charlene was playing with her.

"I've had enough of this dumbass party." She shivered from head to toe, then swung her gaze to the cops huddled at the door. "A dead body was the last straw."

By my estimation, the cops had questioned everyone, and it looked like they were comparing notes. "Hey, if the police didn't order you to stay, then you won't hear it from me. *Hasta la vista*, baby. Don't let the door hit you on the way out."

"Humph. You'd love that, wouldn't you, Valentine? Well, you in your little pink tutu can stay and do your stupid sleuthing. I've got better things to do with my time." She turned on her heels and stomped toward the exit.

I did an overstated plié to her back, refraining from also giving her a scissor kick with my foot. Thankfully, I felt the warmth of my friends close in on me.

"Is she always this charming?" Merry rested her hands on her hips and shook her head.

I took a calming breath. "Charming with a hard *Ch*."

"Why is she leaving?" Kate turned her head from Candace's retreating form to me.

I wanted to say that it was a full moon tonight, which meant Candace wouldn't be the only witch traveling the airways. But I settled for a gentler reply. "Because Candace doesn't believe in hanging around when things go sour." I gazed at Amber's last resting place. "And nothing like a corpse to sour things."

Franki tapped her Italian boot on the tile, eyes narrowed. "I say *arrivederci*, baby. We've got enough suspects without a party crasher adding to the mix."

I agreed and filled them in on Candace's revelation. "Did any of you notice the mustard stains on Stanley's jacket? Or water stains?"

Nonchalantly, all four of us turned our heads and gave a sleuth-eyed stare at Stanley jerking his too-large jacket around on his shoulders, eyes flitting across the room like a weasel. He brought another cream puff to his mouth and fastened his eyes on the yellow stains on his sleeve. A look of horror crossed his face, and he dropped his arm, bouncing the cream puff across the carpet. Then he grabbed a napkin, turned his back, and scrubbed his sleeve.

What was that all about? Was Candace right? Did Stanley have a part in Babette's disappearance? Perhaps he'd pointed the finger at Rock to remove suspicion from himself.

"My money's on *him*." Franki snorted with distaste. "Hell, my money's on everyone...except you three." She paused and glimpsed toward the lobby. "Back to what I wanted to tell you. It's been such a crazy night I can't remember if I even shared the disturbing picture that greeted me when I arrived."

We leaned in, none of us wanting to miss the disturbing picture.

"Amber and Charlie were making out in the elevator."

Three sets of brows hiked up, eyes all on our tall friend.

She nodded at us. "At first, I wasn't sure if the guy *was* Charlie. I even considered Rock since he'd sauntered into the party room after I'd arrived, which would've given him time to pull himself together after that disgusting interlude." Her beautiful cat-lined eyes scanned the bar. "But Mo confirmed it. It was indeed our handsome groom-to-be locking lips with Amber."

"Ha!" Merry lifted her chin. "So the scum was actively two-timing on Babette. I knew he was a complete jerk! I should've used those zip ties on *him*...in a more alarming location."

I gulped at that, recalling the time I'd wrapped the perm rod around murderer Ziggy Stoaks's family jewels. I knew these three would understand my zealousness for catching a felon. But even *I* had to admit the story of how I caught Ziggy was ludicrous.

Blessedly, Kate spoke up before I embarrassed myself by sharing that experience. "Charlie admitted as much to me that he was involved with Amber. At least he called her his ex. Obviously he meant ex-citing distraction from Babette." Her swollen hands curled into fists. "The worm! He was even more interested in who *we* all were than worrying about where his fiancée might be. The snake."

A grin crept up Merry's face. "Which is he? A worm or a snake?"

Kate pursed her lips, clearly fuming inside at Charlie's behavior. "Far as I'm concerned, it's the same family. He's nothing more than a slithering, spineless reptile."

*"Upon his belly he shalt go and eat dust all the days of his life.* Genesis 3:14." Yow. Who knew I could rattle off Bible scripture like that? Of course, I may have reworked the pronouns a bit.

"Amen," Kate offered. "Meanwhile, he wanted *me* to talk to Zelda."

"Because?" I asked.

"Charlie said Zelda hated Amber for botching some St. Paddy's Day gig that Zelda had lined up for Babette. I guess Zelda lost a lot of money because of Amber."

"Sounds like a good motive for murder to me."

Franki's mouth went tight. "No wonder Zelda got touchy when I asked if she had a motive to kill Amber."

"Let's not forget the *Frozen* sisters," Merry added, spying Chelsea and Charlene over her shoulder. "I think they literally had the Snow Queen for a mother. I don't know how Charlie escaped the frosty gene, but I have to admit he is the softest of the three."

"Maybe that's an act," Franki muttered.

"Yeah." Merry's chuckle came out grimly. "The sisters see themselves in line for the crown, although who'd wear it is up for dispute. But one thing is certain. They see Charlie as king. In other words, Amber wasn't fit to lick his boots."

She leaned in and lowered her voice. "They denied anything to do with Amber's death and instead pointed fingers at *us*. I can't tell if they're lying or scared."

"Probably lying *and* scared." Franki slapped her hobo bag on the table by us. "Is that what the detective was grilling you about? Your relationship with Amber?"

Merry gave a carefree shrug. "Yeah, my relationship all of thirty minutes. I guess we've all given a statement by now. Which leads me back to the groom-to-be. When he first got here, he told me he was in hedge funds. Was he bragging to any of you about his power job?"

Kate did a double headshake that said, *Say what?* "I heard him tell Rock he was a financial advisor."

"That's interesting," Franki said. "When I pressed Rock on how long he'd been a bartender, he admitted to lying on his résumé because he needed money for a hand-modeling portfolio. Maybe Charlie smelled an opportunity."

I added my findings. "I overheard him tell Candace earlier that he was in banking."

"Seems the scum has a veritable scummy background," Merry concluded.

Kate placed her hand on Merry's wrist. "What's even more scummy is that Charlie told me Babette only took the job at Higgly Piggly because they needed money for their wedding."

"Looks like we've got a liar in our midst," Merry said. "Sounds like he's broke and leaning on the bride to carry the financial weight of the wedding."

Franki stared from Merry to Kate to me. "Which brings me to what Mo disclosed ten minutes ago. As if we're not already knee-deep in suspects, this will knock your socks off."

"What is it?" Kate had been doing left-handed lazy circles on her belly, but she absently picked up speed.

Franki dropped the bomb without batting an eye. "Babette was here earlier."

"What?" we said in unison.

"Where, here?" I asked.

"*Here* here. At the hotel." She put her palms up. "Mo swore on his mother's grave it's the truth. Although, what woman could have ever conceived him is beyond me."

"Like I said earlier..." Kate's voice hushed to a whisper. "Charlie had also suggested to me that Babette was here."

We took a moment to digest this, each of us evidently adding two and two.

I couldn't wrap my mind around it. "You're saying Babette could've snuck in at some point and poisoned the chocolates?"

"Why not?" Franki asked. "I don't know her like you three, but we have to face facts it's a possibility. And she does have that pharmaceutical bag in her room."

I ran my thumb across my manicured nails, thinking this through. "If Amber died from the chocolates, and the chocolates had been poisoned, who's to say it was Babette who tainted them? She didn't even know the Ghirardellis were there."

Kate ogled us. "Unless Charlie let her know about them when I'd given them to him."

"But how did Babette know Charlie would give them to Amber—if that's what happened? Or were the poisoned chocolates meant for Charlie?" I shook my head. "Seems far-fetched to think of Babette as a murderer. Plus, I know her. I refuse to believe it."

"Me, too," Kate said. "We were super close in college. A person's ethics and true personality wouldn't change like that."

Franki shrugged and rolled her stare to Merry.

"Don't look at *me*," Merry said. "I got outed from the CIA because the Vice President of the United States had a grudge against my dad. Now I lead a troop of Girl Scouts. Go figure."

"You must have an opinion," Franki said. "You've seen enough in your line of work to get a feel for who's guilty and who's innocent."

"I was just starting out in the CIA when I met Babette, so I didn't really have the training yet." She did an up-and-down thing with her eyebrows. "Far as I knew, she was solid. True, people can change, and if driven to it I guess anyone can commit murder. But Babette? I don't know."

Franki blew out a sigh. "Well, if the news of her being here doesn't set off any alarms, when I was in her room, I found this." She hauled from her bag a pad of paper with *Niagara Collateral* imprinted on it. "It was between the nightstand and the bed."

"What?" Kate gawked at the pad. "That could belong to anyone."

Merry took the pad from Franki and studied the name. "One thing I can tell you, I passed that place on the way to the hotel. It's the reigning pawnshop in Niagara Falls."

"I figured as much." Franki whipped out her phone and clicked away. "Yep. Niagara Collateral. Number one pawnshop this side of the border."

Something about all this didn't feel right. If Babette had noted the name of that pawnshop—and that was a big if—the question was why. I tipped toward Merry and studied the curved letters distinctly etched through the imprint. "As much as I hate to admit it, that's Babette's writing all right. No one made those extra swirls on an *N* like her, or the extremely long, sharp downstroke."

Kate studied it alongside me. "Yikes. I agree. Babette always had the most unique handwriting. Flowery yet intense."

I pushed down the panic that was fighting to surface. "Hold on." I spread my hands wide, my glittery ring sparkling in the dim light. "Franki, you're a private investigator. Merry"—I shifted my gaze to our carefree friend—"you're ex-CIA." I tapped my chest. "I'm, for lack of a better word, an amateur sleuth."

Kate's eyes enlarged, implying she made the connection. "And

I'm working on getting my PI license. Oh no," she rushed on. "Do you think there's a reason we were all invited to Babette's party?" Her eyes grew even bigger, if that was possible.

"Maybe she knew she'd need our help." It was better than thinking the worst, that we'd been duped.

"Or were we set up?" Kate mimicked my thoughts.

"Let's not get ahead of ourselves." Merry handed the pad back to Franki. "Maybe Babette was trading in something."

"Like what?" Franki looked from the pad to her phone, to us. "Cuban cigars?"

"Hey, it happens." Merry propped back against a chair and folded her arms in front. "You'd be surprised what gets smuggled these days, from exotic birds to monkey testicles." Her lips went across in a straight line. "You do not want to know about that. Trust me."

"I still don't like the feeling that we might be pawns in this case," Kate said.

We all gave an uncomfortable nod in agreement. Just then, I caught Stanley tiptoeing past the table where I'd placed Babette's pink bag, and slink out of the room. The unease already nagging me instantly compounded, and something inside told me to follow him.

I looked from Stanley to where his cocktail glass rested on the bar, to the cops. Hmm. Maybe they could run his prints. Anyone with suspicious stains on his coat and who acted this jittery had to be hiding something.

"I'll be back in a minute," I told the others, my gaze already zooming in on the pink bag.

Merry winked at me. "You sure you're not calling it a night? Things are just getting exciting."

"Ha. No. I want to take Babette's gift up to my room. It's clear she's not joining the party, and I don't want it lost or stolen." It was a half-truth, but I needed to see what Mr. Higgly Piggly was up to. If it was *no good*, I preferred to go alone and not put the others in danger.

I strolled over to the cream puff he'd sent rolling, picked it up, and pitched it in a nearby waste bin. I made sure no one had noticed me, then wandered to the bar and snatched Stanley's glass with a pair of tweezers I'd scooped from my bag. With the ease of a model on the catwalk, I sashayed past everyone in their private groups, nipped the pink bag from the table, and sauntered toward the exit. *Valentine, you're so sly you could steal the* Mona Lisa *in plain sight.*

I approached Detective van der Donk standing at the exit, waited for him to finish talking to another cop, then held out the glass to him.

"No thanks," he said. "I don't drink when I'm on duty."

I grinned. He might not have Romero's sexy charm, but the guy had a sense of humor. Despite being grilled by him earlier on Amber's murder, I was growing to like him. "I thought you might want to run the prints on this glass that Babette's boss used."

He looked at the tweezers pinching the glass in my hand, then narrowed an eye on me. "You're Valentine Beaumont, right? Beautician and lady friend of Detective Michael Romero."

"In the flesh." I curtsied, then straightened, that last part catching me by surprise. "How do you know about Romero? We only spoke for five minutes."

He chuckled warmly. "Hazards of the job." He grabbed a hanky from his pocket and took the glass from me. "Seems your reputation precedes you."

I felt myself blush but wasn't going to ask what he was referring to. By now, the entire east coast was quite familiar with my perm-rod-to-the-genitals debacle. "I'll take that as a compliment."

He gave me a nod, eyeing my flat iron that was sticking out of my bag. "You should. My daughter's your size, but you wouldn't catch her jumping a felon. What's more, she wouldn't know what to do with a flat iron other than pamper her hair."

He studied the room, then landed his wizened gaze back on me. "When Romero worked in vice here in New York, we'd had occasion to team up together. He's tough. Street smart. And has an impeccable reputation. He's also a wiseass. But I like him."

"That makes two of us." My grin widened.

He grunted in a friendly manner. "And why do you suspect Stanley of any wrongdoing?"

I didn't miss a beat. "Water spots and mustard stains."

"Am I supposed to understand this?"

I gave him the edited version of what I'd seen. "I don't know if he knew Amber. But he knows Babette, and she's missing. I thought it couldn't hurt for you to run his prints."

"Anything else you'd like for us to do?"

Sheesh. And *Romero's* the wiseass.

"No." I hitched both bags over my shoulder. "That's about it."

Another cop interrupted us, and I took the opportunity to sneak out of the room before anyone asked where I was going. I hurried down the hall, searching for Stanley. Darn. Where did he go? The men's bathroom was ahead on the left. If Stanley wasn't in there, he'd still be walking the long hallway.

I passed a supply room just before the men's bathroom when an idea struck. I backed up and glared at the sign under *Supply Room* marked *Staff Only*. Right. When did that ever stop me? I gripped the doorknob, thinking I might have to get creative again and break in like I did for Babette's room, which reminded me I had to dispose of her key card. Last thing I needed was to be implicated in a murder as Franki suggested. But first things first.

Luckily, the door was unlocked. My nose twitched out of nervousness, but I ignored the warning. I'd wait in here until Stanley exited the bathroom. It was a perfect setup.

I crept into the dimly lit room and took a brief look around. It was bigger than I'd anticipated. Bar napkins, bath amenities, and laundry supplies lined several tall shelves. Buckets, mops, rubber gloves, and cleansers padded another wall. The disinfectant smell reminded me of my parents' house. Ha. Who was I fooling? Mr. Clean couldn't keep up with my mother.

Leaving the light off, I quietly shut the door and put my ear to it, hoping to hear Stanley make his move. Thinking better of my position, I knelt and peered at the crack under the door. If I didn't hear him leave the men's room, I'd see his shadow from under the door.

I was congratulating myself on how clever I was when I heard a rustling sound behind me. Before I could turn around, a pair of hands swung around my face and covered my nose and mouth, half lifting me off the floor.

"Mff-mff!" I dropped both bags to the ground. Instinctively, I squirmed with all my might and tried to pry the hands away from my nose, the fear of suffocating overcoming me.

The grip tightened and my pulse pounded like a gong in my ear. For a terrifying moment, I pictured Rock using his muscular arms to smother me. Who else would be in the supply closet?

"Shhh!" the voice whispered down my neck.

I hiccupped back panic and reached into the bag closest to me, clutching the first thing I felt. A small glass bottle. Aha! The mini champagne I'd packed in Babette's bag.

Between the dim lighting and me struggling to get loose, my attacker didn't seem to notice the bottle or me twisting off the plastic cork. I gave it a shake and aimed it over my right ear. Suddenly, there was a *POP*. The cork flew past my shoulder along with a spray of bubbly.

*Whunk.*

"Aaaaah!" my attacker wailed and dropped his hands from my face.

I bent forward and gasped for air, then scrambled to my feet and spun around. "*Stanley!*"

He fell back and shook his soaked bald head, his hand cupping the right side of his face. "Are you *inthane?*" he spit out. "You got me in the eye with that thing."

I was still catching my breath. "You scared me to death!" I gripped the empty champagne bottle tightly by the neck and hovered over him. "What are you doing in here?"

He cowered under me. "I thaw you following me."

"So?"

"You need to back off."

"I'll back off, Stanley, when I know what happened to Babette. Now tell me why you were slinking out of the party room."

"I had to make a phone call."

"Who were you calling?"

"My dry cleaner."

I moved in, bottle poised. "Why call a dry cleaner this late on a Saturday night?"

"Aaah!" he yelped. "Becauth...becauth they didn't get the stains off my jacket."

I glared down at his mustard stains, the smell no competition for the cleaning agents in the room. "Are you sure?"

"About what?"

"That those aren't fresh stains? Ones you might've obtained when strangling Babette?"

No one said Babette had been strangled, and I didn't know where I was going with all this, but I wanted to see if he'd crack. The faster I ripped into the pipsqueak, the more chances he'd slip up.

"Aaah!" he yelped again, bending back. "Okay. Okay. I wathn't making a phone call."

"Naughty, naughty, Stanley. It's not nice to lie." Listen to me. Like I'd never told a fib before. "Then what were you doing?"

He glared up at me through his uncovered eye as if there was no winning. "Hath anyone told you you're intruthive? And difficult?"

Romero once told me I was difficult. Or was it twice? Well, I wasn't always difficult. "Stop evading the question!"

He huffed out air, then hauled out a syringe from inside his coat pocket. "If you muth know, I'm diabetic. I didn't want to inject my inthulin in public. Geeth, can't a guy have any privathy?"

I stared at the syringe in his hand. Just like the ones in Babette's pharmaceutical bag. Was he telling the truth? Since all indicators pointed to Fentanyl as being the lethal drug that killed Amber, had Stanley found a way into Babette's room and used a syringe to inject the drug into the chocolates? If so, the question was how.

Did he steal her key card when she was at work today? Suppose he snuck into her room with a half-assed plan to hurt her. Then what if he saw the chocolates? If he poisoned them, it would follow that Babette was the intended victim. So how did Amber get them?

"If I find out you're lying, I'll play Terminator on your hair, and you'll wake up one morning with the rest of your curls on your pillow." I had the products to do it, too. "Got it?"

His bottom lip quivered, but I was on a roll. "Now tell me why you have mustard stains on your coat."

He got to his feet and did a one-handed tug on his jacket, an indignant look on his half-covered face. "Boy, are you relentleth."

I overlooked his lisp and gave an impatient tap on the bottle in my hand.

"All right, already. I gave Babette all thothe complimentary jarth, and when I needed one to go with a hot dog I had to open a dumb packet. Thquirted muthtard all over me. The damn water fountain made it worthe when I tried to clean it off." He frowned. "Why would I want to hurt Babette, anyway? She'th making good money for Higgly Piggly."

He had a point. I swung open the door to the supply room. "Get out of here, Stanley."

He muttered glumly and shuffled back to the party room.

Something needled me about the supply closet as if a finger were tapping me on the shoulder. But I brushed it off. I simply had the heebie-jeebies because of my interaction with Stanley.

I didn't want to waste another minute. I rushed into the ladies' room across the hall. In case Babette's defunct key card could be traced to her, I wiped off my prints, sliced it up with my straight razor and, for good measure, flushed it down the toilet.

I dropped off Babette's bag in my room and ambled back to the party room. There were too many unanswered questions about Babette's disappearance and Amber's murder, but if experience had taught me anything, it was to never omit a clue. At this point, I wasn't sure which clue would help us solve the case. But Merry, Kate, Franki, and I were determined, if not relentless, and if there was one thing I knew for sure, it was that we wouldn't give up until this mystery was solved.

# BABETTE

## DIANA ORGAIN

The oxygen seemed sucked out of the room.

*Amber, murdered?*

Impossible.

My heart clenched and for a moment, the room spun in an awful tilt-a-whirl fashion. I lurched forward and gripped the gray table. Officers Saunders and Jones watched me, giving me the strangest sensation in my chest.

Then it hit me.

*This is a joke!*

I slapped the table. "Ha! You got it! Good one. First the terrorist stuff, now a fake murder." I scanned the ceiling and saw a discreetly mounted motion-sensor camera. I pointed to it. "Are we streaming live on YouTube? Is Zelda behind this?"

Detective Bourbon glared at me. "No ma'am. We are *not* live streaming. Do you care to tell us who Zelda is?"

I looked frantically from his face to Officers Saunders and Jones. No one was laughing.

*Oh no.*

"Amber is really dead?" I stuttered.

"Can you please tell me, ma'am, about your whereabouts this evening?"

Adrenaline shot through my leg, which bounced so violently it shook the table.

Detective Bourbon put a hand on the table to steady it and stop it from rattling. My leg, however, did not stop. Despite his attempts, the table rocked forward, then back, and pitched my coffee cup onto its side, sloshing the hot liquid right onto my lap.

I sprang to my feet. "Ouch!"

"Sit!" Detective Bourbon barked.

"I…uh…sorry." I sat, chagrined and soaked.

He fanned a hand at me to answer his question.

I gulped. "I was working. You know that. Not for the Monkey…Monkey Fist or whatever, but for Higgly Piggly."

He glanced down at the file in his hand. "Right. Listen, I understand this news is upsetting, but if there's anything you can tell us, it would benefit your case."

*My case!*

I had a case? My life flashed before my eyes. I was never going to walk down the aisle. I was never going to have kids. I was never to be a star.

*Why had I gone back to the hotel?*

They knew, didn't they? Mo had blabbed, and the police knew I'd been to the hotel earlier.

They were toying with me. All that nonsense about a terrorist association—that was to get me off guard. I needed to focus.

*Did I need to call a lawyer? Charlie?*

Detective Bourbon rapped on the table with the file folder. "Miss Lang, do you have anything you want to tell us?"

"About what?" I squeaked.

Bourbon narrowed his eyes at me. "About Amber. About who might want her dead?"

I swallowed past the dry lump in my throat. "I can't think of a single person who wouldn't want her dead…except…"

"Except who?" Officer Jones asked.

It burned my soul to admit it.

"Charlie. He's still in love with her."

WHAT FELT LIKE A LIFETIME LATER, but in reality was only about fifteen minutes, I stood outside the police station, back in my hot dog costume because the police had refused my request to keep the coffee-soaked jail jumper. What should've been one of the best nights of my life had turned into the worst.

It wasn't the embarrassment of the hot dog costume, nor the fact that my Mini Cooper Wienermobile was still at the Falls and I was stranded, nor the dishonor of being mistaken for a terrorist. It was the sheer and utter humiliation of realizing that Charlie was still in love with Amber.

That's why she'd been at the party.

Charlie had invited her.

They'd never broken up.

The wind buffeted my face and my belly, the two places exposed in this ridiculous outfit. I squinted from the wind and blinked back the tears that burned my eyes.

How could I have been so *stupid*!

Suddenly a soul-freeing scream burst from my body. "I'm going to kill you, Charlie!"

A chuckle from behind startled me. I swung around to find Officer Jones.

"Wow!" She blinked in astonishment. "You got some lungs!"

"Thanks. I'm a singer."

"Yeah? You should be on Broadway. You got that look."

I stood a little straighter, hot dog costume and all. "Really?"

She nodded. "Absolutely. But hey, a word of advice, please don't stand outside a police station and scream your intentions of murder. Especially when you're implicated in an on-going murder investigation."

I cringed. "It was a figure of speech. I'm not actually going to kill him, but I'm certainly not marrying him."

She nodded. "Good. You deserve better. Need a lift back to your ride?"

I did, but the last thing I wanted to do was drive the Wiener-mobile. I chewed my lip. "Actually, can you call me a cab? I lost my phone, and tonight's just not my night."

She rapidly tapped at the screen of her mobile. "I don't know. At least you're not stuck behind bars." She flashed me a smile that I couldn't muster the energy to match. Her smile turned into a thin line. "And all things considered, it was a worse night for Amber."

I froze. She was right. Goosebumps rose on the back of my neck, and I had the strange thought that maybe missing my own party had saved my life.

Within moments, a cab rounded the corner. Officer Jones raised a hand to hail it over.

I sighed. "How am I supposed to fit in the back?"

"Yeah." She chuckled. "It's going to be tight."

The cab rolled to a stop in front of me and, to fit, I horizon-tally dove face down into the backseat.

I heard Officer Jones chuckle again. "Goodbye, Babette. I'll never forget you."

Groaning, I said, "This is not how I want to be remembered."

The driver swiveled around and mumbled, "Where to, kid?"

I strained to look at him. He had an unlit cigar in his mouth.

"Niagara Collateral."

"You gotta be kidding me? Nice girl like you? What do you want with a pawnshop?"

I harrumphed.

I used to be a nice girl. Tonight, I wasn't so sure. Anyway, what would he know? To him, I was only a hot dog girl.

"Not that it's your business, but I need to get my grandma's bracelet back."

"Ah. Anything for grandma!" He stepped on the gas, and the car lurched forward.

Let me tell you, riding in a speeding car, face down in the backseat, wearing a hot dog costume is no ride in the park. But there was something cathartic about it. By the end of the ride, I'd vowed never to be involved with a man again. In my book, they'd all been lying, cheating scumbags. I'd be better off in a nunnery.

Okay, that was not going to happen. But maybe I could focus on my career. Starting with firing Zelda. I'd gotten nothing but terrible bit parts working with her. Officer Jones was right. I belonged on Broadway. As soon as possible, I'd start auditioning again.

"Here we are, sweetheart. Niagara Collateral."

I slithered on my tummy out of the back door, trying to show a little pride. "Hey, can you do me a favor? Can you wait? I'll only be a minute, and then I need a lift to the Park Avenue Hotel."

"The Park Avenue Hotel, eh? Sure. It's been a popular night for that place. I think there's some rip-roaring bachelorette party going on there."

I ignored him and marched over to the pawnshop. The windows were covered in filth, and the dimly lit entryway gave me pause, but I thought of Grandma Barbie and Johnny "The Mooch" Muccitelli and gripped the door handle.

*Tonight, this very night, Babette is reborn.*

I am no longer a girl who will be stomped on by men. I am my own woman. I am a woman in charge of her destiny. I am ready for my moment!

I pushed open the door, stepped inside, and was promptly boomeranged out as the top of the hot dog costume hit the doorway.

"Ouch!" I whimpered.

"Who's there?" a voice called.

I rubbed at my whiplashed neck. "It's me, Babette Lang. I called earlier. I'm here to pick up my grandmother's heirloom sapphire bracelet."

An elderly man hustled from behind the counter and squinted at me. "What? Babette Long?"

"Lang."

"Yeah. You came by earlier. Geez, your memory must be worse than mine."

"I did not come by earlier."

He frowned. "Sure you did, but you were wearing something else...something normal. It was a little flashy. But nice. What are those sparkly things called? Sequins?" He looked me up and down. "What are you wearing now, dear? Is that the latest fashion?"

I disregarded the slight, but not the sinking feeling in my gut. "Do you have my bracelet?"

He scratched at his nearly bald head. "No. You have it. I gave it to you when you came in the first time." He rushed back to the counter and rustled through his receipts. "See? You even signed for it."

He thrust the paper at me, and I saw an entry in barely legible handwriting that read *Babette Long*.

# KATE

## DIANA ORGAIN

*I* waddled as fast as I could to the ladies' room. The fact that it was the last place I'd chatted with Amber bothered me, but I knew I couldn't make it in time to my room upstairs. I swung open the door and hurled myself into a stall past the large lemon-colored settee that still screamed Amber in tears.

Someone was in the stall next to me, but it hardly registered. I just needed some relief from the bladder pressure.

Had I really downed that many club sodas? Or was this just the twins' revenge for being on my feet so long?

The stall next to me rattled as its occupant exited, and then an unmistakably raspy deep voice called out. "Is that you, Chels?"

*Zelda.*

Before I could answer, she said, "I can't believe Amber's dead. I mean, I guess it shouldn't surprise me…" She continued to speak but also flipped on the tap to wash her hands, and I could only catch every few words. "…jealous…over…cost…floozy…"

The tap water sounded as loud as Niagara Falls! Geez, why did this rundown hotel have to have the best water pressure!

She mercifully turned off the tap.

"Sorry, but it's true…" Then the sound of the hand dryer!

*Seriously?*

"I won't tell…" The dryer turned off and she said, "Well?"

I opened the door to the stall and caught her clamping her teeth back into her mouth. "Sorry. I'm not Chelsea, but don't worry. I couldn't make out a thing over the noise of the water and dryer."

She chuckled. "Oh honey, I'm not hiding anything." She turned to the mirror and proceeded to attempt to tame the tangled mess of platinum blonde on her head. I held back a giggle as I thought what my darling husband, Jim, would say about Zelda. He'd call her hair a fright wig for sure.

As I watched Zelda fuss, I swear the whole mop of hair heaved to the left.

*It was a wig!*

Not that I had anything against wigs. As a former theater major, I loved all things costume, but if you were going to parade around in a wig, why not choose an attractive one?

I bit my lip. I knew enough about the world to not poke a bear.

I washed my hands in the sink and said innocently, "I gather you didn't much like Amber."

"I think the only one who will miss her is Charlie…and maybe Chelsea. They were buddies. Everyone else didn't like her. Me especially. She cost me a lot of money when she ratted out Babette for the St. Paddy's gig. What nerve! Did you know Babette's mother was Irish?"

"No, I didn't."

Zelda waved her hand about. "Well, maybe it was her mother's mother…or her mother's mother's mother? I can't recall. But there was Irish lineage there. That counts for something. To think we would've made that up. It's unfathomable really. Losing the St. Paddy's gig was one thing, but"—she thumped her chest and the seventeen bangles on her wrist jangled—"it cost my reputation. I tell you, I'm not sorry that floozy is dead."

She turned on a heel and marched out the door.

I dried my hands and flopped onto the velvet settee. I propped up my feet and contemplated kicking off my shoes. No. If I took them off, I'd never get them back on.

Better to focus on something else rather than the uncomfortableness of pregnancy.

*Amber.*

Who wanted her dead?

According to Franki, Charlie had been seen making out with Amber. He was distraught over her death. Obviously still in love with her. I'd mistaken all the clues he'd given me in our earlier conversation. He wasn't in love with Babette.

*What a shame.*

Given that Franki had also reported Babette had somehow snuck into the hotel without us spotting her, she was the prime suspect. If she knew about the affair, then she had motive.

But I couldn't believe that of Babette. She was one of the sweetest friends I'd had in college. There was just no way. While I sat contemplating things, my mobile buzzed. I dug it out of my purse and glanced at the screen.

Mom.

I happily answered the call. "Hey, Mom. What's going on?"

"Just calling to check in and see how you're feeling. Are you having fun with Babette?"

I brought Mom up to speed on the entire night.

"How did this girl die?" she asked.

"We don't know exactly. Opioid overdose. Babette has a bag of pharmaceuticals in her room."

Mom sucked in her breath. "Oh my! That *is* bad. Have you talked to Babette at all?"

"No. She's totally MIA. Her boss was here and said she had to work late, but I don't know. One of the other gals, a PI out of New Orleans, found a note in her room about a pawnshop. I think Babette may be trying to recover her grandmother's heirloom bracelet."

"Hmm. If Babette isn't there, though, how would she be able to give the woman an overdose?"

"That's the thing. Everyone is assuming Amber died from eating the chocolates I brought for Babette."

Mom tsked. "My goodness! The Ghirardelli chocolates?"

"Yup."

"I hope they're not thinking you had anything to do with this!"

"How could I? I don't even know Amber."

"Right, of course." Mom sighed. "I wish I could be with you. Call me with any updates. I'm going to go ice my shoulder."

"Ice your shoulder? What happened? Did you hurt yourself?"

"Nothing to worry about, darling. Galigani and I got matching tattoos."

Galigani was retired from the SFPD, my PI mentor and Mom's boyfriend.

"*What?*"

She chuckled. "I'd never gotten one and neither had he. So we just decided for fun to get one."

"Mom! I can't believe it! You're sixty years old!"

"Don't be ageist, Kate. There's no age limit on fun."

"Ugh. Whatever, I didn't mean that. It's just…" I was about to say it wasn't like her, but that wasn't true. It was exactly like her to get a tattoo. It was unlike Galigani, that was for sure, but my mother could be very convincing.

The door to the restroom squeaked open, and I said, "Gotta go, Mom. I'll talk to you later."

I looked up to see Chelsea rush past me. She didn't acknowledge me but hustled to a stall and locked the door.

I put away my phone and made to get up, but hesitated.

*Lots of secrets are shared in the ladies' room.*

I waited. Within moments, Chelsea exited the stall and washed her hands.

"I'm so sorry for your loss," I said.

She turned to me, her eyes red-rimmed. "My loss? More like Charlie's loss. It's no secret. He was in love with Amber."

I sighed. "Why is he marrying Babette then?"

She shook her head. "Beats me. I told him over and over, 'You've got the wrong one, Charlie. Wrong one.'" She dried her hands. "You think he listened? Men never listen, but honestly, I couldn't believe he asked Babette. I mean, why? She's a wannabe actress, a second-rate singer, and a poor salesperson. She's not even that pretty."

"She's my friend," I said. "She's got a huge heart. Charlie would be lucky to have her."

Chelsea breezed past me. "*Pff.* Whatever. Like I said, wrong one!"

She exited the restroom, and I found myself relieved that she'd gone.

Still her words echoed...wrong one...wrong one.

*What if...*

I cradled my head between my hands.

*Think, Kate, think!*

These pregnancy hormones were killers. No sooner would an idea strike than I get fog brain.

*Wrong one.* What was it about that sentiment that set me off?

Then it hit me. Everyone assumed Amber had been poisoned with the chocolates I brought. The chocolates intended for Babette.

What if the killer had targeted the wrong victim?

# MERRY

## LESLIE LANGTRY

"*A*nd this is called *goat with gastrointestinal issues.*" Valentine and Franki gave me strange looks. "Yeah, well," I explained, "Chechens aren't very creative with naming things."

I doubled over, swore loudly in Chechen, and threw a table knife underhanded at the dartboard. It buried itself in the foam just outside the bullseye with a satisfying *thunk*. There were no darts. Mo said they'd been stolen sometime in 1982 and were never replaced. That was the last knife. Time to move on to the forks...

This place was starting to get to me. Sure, I'd been stuck in rooms with a killer before, but nowhere near as depressing as this place—and that includes the time I was trapped in a dilapidated shack with a murderous mouse juggler in a remote village in Turkmenistan. I survived by throwing him through one of the walls. I miss throwing people through walls. It's so satisfying.

Why was I throwing cheap, crap flatware? We were discussing the case so far and trying to figure out what to do when I suggested something to take our minds off things for a moment.

Valentine, Franki, and I were looking around for some forks as Kate walked over.

"Guys..." She looked both left and right. "Turns out, Charlie really loved Amber. I don't know why he's marrying Babette. Probably for the money."

Valentine looked peeved. "Guess we figured as much. Poor Babette. Someone's going to have to tell her when she gets here. I volunteer."

"She definitely deserves someone better than him," Kate agreed.

"Can I throw Charlie through a wall?" I asked the others. I hadn't thrown anyone through a wall in years. It would be fun! My aim might be off, though. Maybe a window would be better.

Franki grinned. "Charlie might get you for assault, but the three of us can say you didn't do it."

"I can trip," I suggested. "And make it look like an accident."

"I like this idea." Valentine stuck out her sparkly heel in my direction. "I could even be the reason you tripped."

"That would work." I gave a devious nod. "Accidental tripping on purpose is one of the first things we learn at the Farm during CIA training. That and how to impersonate Reba McEntire." The women stared at me. "What? You'd be surprised how useful that is. Reba fits in naturally for any occasion."

"And that's not all," Kate continued. "Zelda told me, and Chelsea confirmed it, that Chelsea and Amber were good friends. She doesn't even like Babette!"

"So that woman lied to me," I said evenly.

"Chelsea..." Valentine started, but I cut her off.

"Nope." I held up my hand. "She's *that woman* now. *That woman* lied to me, so she doesn't get to have a name. Like Voldemort or Nixon." I didn't like it when people lied to me.

Maybe I should throw Chelsea *and* her brother through a wall. Seriously, I could use the activity. I hadn't done much all night. The exercise would be welcome.

"What if Amber wasn't the target?" Kate tapped her chin. "What if it was Babette? That's who the chocolates were for."

I held up my index finger. "And if Charlie's sister preferred that her slimy brother marry Amber, but Charlie wanted to go through with marrying Babette, it wouldn't be a stretch to imagine his sister considering the idea of murdering her. She probably thought she was saving Charlie from marrying a woman he wasn't in love with. She was hoping she could blame one of us for it. I still can't get over the fact that she made me handle the guest list when the only person I knew was Babette."

"It's the same for all of us." Franki shrugged. "I barely even knew Babette."

"Someone needs to talk to *that woman*...again." Valentine aimed an eyebrow at me.

Franki nodded at that and shifted her stare at me as well. "You're the only one who's developed a rapport with Chelsea... except for Kate just now in the bathroom. Maybe you'll catch her off guard."

I looked at the three of them, and they all bobbed their heads. "Fine. I'll do it."

For as much as I didn't want to talk to her ever again, I grabbed a piece of cake and a fork and joined the liar at her empty table. Time to play *bad cop*.

"See this fork?" I held it up as the woman glowered at me for sitting without asking first. "There are thirty-seven and a half things I can do to hurt you with it."

"And a half?" She snorted. "That sounds stupid."

I pointed the fork at her. "The half is when you use it with a salt spoon, but I don't have one of those on me, do I?" I began spinning the fork through my fingers. "Forks are great because they can cause a lot of pain with minimal markings." I picked up a piece of cake and stabbed the fork through it until it stood upright.

"Why are you telling me this?" Chelsea's eyes darted around

the room.

"Because you lied to me." My eyes drilled into hers. "I don't like it when people lie to me. It's not very nice."

She gave me a startled look. "What did I lie to you about?"

"You said you *hated* Amber. You wanted me to get rid of her. And now someone has. And I just found out that you're in mourning for one of your best friends. Sound familiar?"

For a moment, the woman looked defiant. She was considering sticking to her story. Then she saw Kate watching her. She had to know that I'd been told.

I pulled the fork out of the cake and drove it through the tablecloth and into the cheap wood of the table until it stood upright on its own. "You're not thinking of lying to me again, are you?"

Damaging the table didn't bother me. If they spotted it at the end of the night, the table would just have four small holes in it. I was pretty sure they wouldn't care. They'd just throw a tablecloth over it that had been bought at a fire sale from an ethnic cleansing for their next event, which would probably be something like Sarcasm Anonymous, or the Brotherhood of Depressed Clowns, or a group of insurance adjusters.

Chelsea sat back in her chair and sulked. "I don't want Charlene to know, okay? She loathes Amber, and if she thought I was friends with her, she'd never talk to me again."

"You say that like it would be a bad thing." After a bit of a struggle, I pulled the fork out and cut into the cake. These would definitely work great on the dartboard.

She shrugged. "She's my sister."

I never had a sister, so I guess I couldn't really understand that.

"Do you think your sister killed Amber?" I asked without missing a beat.

This time, her jaw dropped open. "What? No! Charlene may be the angriest woman in town, but she wouldn't hurt a fly!"

"Yes, but she's smart enough to poison someone." I leaned in. "And she had a bookmark that had *Fentanyl* written on it."

Chelsea literally turned green. But that could be due to the fact that I was eating off the same fork I'd driven into the table. It was a questionable decision on my part, but come on…it's *cake*.

"And what's all this about Charlie not even being in love with Babette?" I wondered aloud. "Maybe I should take my fork show on the road to the table that's propping him up?"

The woman's hand shot out and touched my arm. "No, please don't do that. He's fragile enough. Can't you see that?"

When the groom-to-be saw that we were looking at him, he scowled and gave us a rude gesture.

"Does he usually flip you the bird?" I asked.

"That was for you," Chelsea said icily. "You and your three friends. You aren't supposed to be investigating." Her anger wove through her words. She wasn't as afraid of me now. "This is for the cops."

I sat back. "Maybe Amber wasn't the intended victim."

"What?" Chelsea shrieked.

"It occurs to us *meddling kids*," I waved in the direction of my friends, "that it's possible that someone meant for Babette to eat the chocolates." I waited for that to sink in before continuing. "Which would really be devastating to the murderer if they killed their best friend instead of the person the poison was meant for."

*That woman* was livid. "You don't know anything! Amber's dead! She's not supposed to be dead. She's supposed to marry Charlie. Not that Babette bimbo. Now, go away! Let the police handle this. And I'm not saying another word to you without a lawyer present."

Even though I was across the room from the dartboard, I checked to make sure the coast was clear, then took the fork, and flung it over my shoulder. A gasp went up telling me I hit a pretty good score. "That's a new one. I just made it up. It's called *It's hard to lie with a fork flying toward your head*."

The look on her face was priceless, even though I felt the name of that act was a bit wordy. I'd have to work on that and my aim. Disappointingly, I only hit the inner triple ring.

I rejoined the girls. "Guess what? *That woman* says what she told Kate is true. Chelsea really liked Amber. She also thinks we should feel sorry for two-timing Charlie over there."

I didn't feel sorry for him. He noticed the four of us glaring in his general direction and yelled, "What's your problem?"

Turning back to the group, I went on. "And, I mentioned the Fentanyl bookmark and asked if the killer meant to kill Babette, but *that woman* blew her top and lawyered up."

"Hey!" Charlie was on his feet. "You women are ridiculous! Stop asking people stuff!"

I locked my eyes on the faithless groom. And when Mo walked in front of me seconds later, I pinched Mo's right elbow without taking my eyes off Charlie. The hotel clerk immediately dropped to the floor unconscious. Charlie blanched and looked away.

"Relax," I said to Kate, who was attempting to kneel down and check on Mo. "He's fine. Fortunately, the nerve in the elbow is weaker, so he'll only be out a second or two." I looked at Mo. "Do I seem a bit too angry and intimidating? I think I've had too much sugar."

"Where do the sisters stand on the suspect list?" Valentine asked as she helped Kate up.

Franki shook her head. "Charlene is still in the running with that Fentanyl bookmark. But I don't know about Chelsea. It seems unlikely that she'd kill Amber."

Kate rubbed her back. "We can't rule out the idea that Chelsea might've poisoned them to kill Babette."

"I think we're getting close, guys." I emptied the rest of the bottle I'd swiped earlier into my wine glass and started to drink when two identical men walked in the door.

"Oh no." I groaned as FBI Agents Winter and Summer looked

around. "What are those idiots doing here?" I'd had dealings with these two before.

"You know those guys?" Franki rolled her eyes. "They look like they dress from the FBI playbook."

"Unfortunately, yes," I answered. "I thought they were still stationed in Omaha."

Both men spotted me at once and made a beeline in my direction.

"Well if it isn't the Possum Urethra terrorist!" Winter snarled.

"Like I told you before," I grumbled, "I'm not a terrorist."

"The FBI thinks you're a terrorist?" Valentine asked.

"Possum Urethra?" Kate added. "Sounds made up."

"It does," I admitted. "But you'll be as surprised as *I* was that it's a real group."

Winter sneered. "Seems mighty suspicious that *you're* here when we have a Monkey Vagina terrorist group in town."

Huh? Okay, that one had to be made up.

"I'm Agent Winter." Winter introduced them to my crew while eyeing everyone with deep suspicion. "And this is Agent Summer."

Franki's right eyebrow went up. "You're joking."

"The FBI never jokes!" Winter raged.

"That's because they have no sense of humor," I said.

"That's right, Curly Sue!" Winter snapped. "And don't you forget it!"

"I don't think we have *no* sense of humor." Summer frowned. "Agent Spring told a funny joke the other day about an aardvark, a train conductor, and a roll of aluminum foil that was—"

Winter cut his partner off and pulled him aside. "What did I say about contradicting me in front of terrorists?"

"I wasn't exactly contradicting you," Summer said. "I just think you were wrong."

Winter threw his hands in the air. "That's the same thing!"

The two men began gesturing wildly as they screamed at each

other.

"Do you think we should stop them before they get into it?" Kate asked me.

"Nah. This is entertaining," I replied. I kind of wanted to start chanting *Fight! Fight! Fight!*

"Stupid name aside..." Kate chewed her lip. "What's this about a terrorist group in town?"

"Probably nothing." Franki smiled as Winter grabbed Summer's gun and ran around, holding it out of reach.

"That doesn't give me much confidence in the FBI." Valentine bit her perfectly defined lip.

"Most are okay," I declared. "But every now and then, guys like this slip through. We had it in the CIA, too."

"Really?" Kate watched Winter throw an all-out temper tantrum.

"Oh yeah," I assured her. "Every occupation has its morons and jerks. Look at Valentine's friend, Candace."

Valentine burst out laughing.

"This is amusing and all," Franki said. "But what is the FBI doing here? It's a murder, not a national incident or kidnapping."

"It's because of me." Babette appeared out of seemingly nowhere. "Apparently, I'm a member of that monkey terrorist group."

My cell buzzed with a text from Ava from my troop, who was also the first ever mayor of Who's There who was still in elementary school.

*Mrs. Wrath, you may be in violation of permit regulations for the work you're doing at your old house, so I may have to fine you. I think one million dollars sounds fair...*

Ava called me Mrs. Wrath—in fact, my whole troop called me Mrs. Wrath—even before I became a real Mrs.

I threw the phone on the nearest table and joined in the group hug that surrounded Babette. My garage crisis could wait because the missing bachelorette was no longer missing.

# FRANKI

## TRACI ANDRIGHETTI

"What happened to you, Babette?" I asked as I extracted myself from the group hug. Although the real question was *What happened to your hot dog?* The wiener was cocked at a jaunty angle, and the middle had sprouted satiny udders.

Stanley screamed from his stool at the far end of the bar and squeezed his chubby cheeks. "The coth—, coth—, coth—"

Zelda whacked his back.

"Thankth," Stanley said. "That cothtume'th coming out of your pay, Babette."

She put her hands on her hot dog hips. "It's always about the money with you, Stanley. I went from the Falls to the police station to a pawnshop, and I can tell you we've got bigger problems than this costume."

Zelda adjusted her wig. "Yeah, like this party."

Babette puckered smudged red lips at her agent. "That's a terrible thing to say. I can see a lot of effort went into the planning."

My gaze swept the drab room and landed on the candlesticks with hair extensions. *I couldn't.*

Babette sighed. "I just feel awful that my party turned so tragic for Amber."

Zelda shrugged. "I was talking about the clampdown on the food and booze, but now that you mention it, her murder was a downer too."

Pain flickered across Babette's face, and she looked at Rock behind the bar. "Can I please get a drink?"

He pointed a glove at me. "*She* cut everyone off."

I rubbed Babette's bunned shoulder, trying to comfort her for the shock to come. "Because Amber was poisoned, and we're not certain of the source."

"Oh, how horrible."

Merry shot her a look as pointed as the tines on the fork she'd swiped from a nearby table. "It gets worse."

Valentine took Babette's arm. "You might want to have a seat."

"Sit next to me, sweetie." Kate patted the barstool beside her.

There was no easy way to say this, so I decided to blurt it out. "We think the killer used Fentanyl from your work suitcase to poison a box of Ghirardelli chocolates Kate brought for you."

Babette turned the colors of her sparkly mustard-and-relish eyeshadow. "Are you sure? Fentanyl is fairly common." She gestured to Charlene, who'd resumed reading in the corner. "For instance, Charlie's sister was just prescribed Fentanyl for back pain."

Charlene slammed *Moby Dick* shut. "I guess no one mentioned the HIPAA Privacy Rule during your pharmaceutical sales training!"

Chelsea rose from the table she shared with Charlie. "How dare you implicate my sister. You could have poisoned those chocolates yourself. After all, you and Amber were hardly friends."

Babette clenched her fists. "I never even saw those chocolates, and I certainly didn't wish Amber any harm."

"*I* certainly did." Charlene pushed up her glasses. "But after researching Fentanyl's side effects, I never filled the prescription. So you can't pin her murder on me."

That chick was as hard as the *ch* in her name. "Someone in this room killed Amber, and if those chocolates *were* poisoned, then Babette was most likely the intended victim."

All eyes turned to Charlie, who was too much of a coward to get up from the table and face his fiancée. "I didn't kill her."

Babette stayed on her stool, braced by Kate's supportive arm. "I know you didn't, because you loved her. But you did conspire with her to steal my grandmother's bracelet. She claimed it from Niagara Collateral right before the party started."

Gasps arose in the room.

Charlie clenched his hands in a pleading gesture. "Babs, baby, I didn't conspire with her. I swear."

"Don't 'Babs, baby' me. You're the only one who knew I'd been scouring pawnshops for that bracelet."

He wiped sweat from his upper lip. "I admit I mentioned it to Amber, but there was no plot. I'd planned to surprise you with it on our wedding day...just as soon as you made enough money for me to buy it back from the pawnshop."

Valentine huffed. "What a hero."

Charlie angled an angry glance at her before cranking out crocodile tears for his bride-to-be. "Can you forgive me, Babs?"

"Of course I forgive you."

Merry threw up her hands, and I almost threw up my drinks.

"But the engagement is off," Babette said. "You two-timing bum."

Zelda let out a whistle that knocked her teeth askew, and Kate, Merry, Valentine, and I erupted in applause. Charlie burst into very real tears, no doubt over the loss of his meal ticket.

Once the clapping subsided, Valentine gave Babette an affectionate squeeze. "You deserve some pampering after what you've been through." She hauled her bag of beauty tools onto the bar. "Why don't I fix your hair?"

Babette touched the hot dog costume covering her gorgeous mane. "I'd like that, but this headpiece is firmly attached."

"I can fix that, too." Valentine pulled out a straight razor, and Stanley let out a shriek, leaping off his stool. Valentine stared Stanley down, razor high, then told Babette to bend forward. Stanley paled and turned away from what he knew was coming.

Valentine yanked the top of the costume away from Babette's head and sliced off the wiener. "Much better." She smiled at her accomplishment and flung the headpiece onto a nearby table.

Babette straightened, and everyone agreed it was an improvement. Except Stanley. He was head-in-hands, crying like a baby.

Merry gestured for Kate and me to follow her to the dartboard. "Just when you thought the party couldn't get any worse."

"It does," I said.

Kate rubbed her back. "Right? The wedding's off, and Babette's bracelet is evidence in a murder investigation."

Merry tossed the fork. "Where do you guys think the bracelet is?"

"Amber's purse?" Kate guessed.

I chewed my cheek. "I doubt she would've had it on her. Since she picked it up before the party, it's probably stashed here at the hotel, which means we have to find it before it ends up in enemy hands."

Agents Summer and Winter sprang to attention.

"You with Monkey Vagina too?" Summer asked.

"Uh, no, but I've applied to the Bearded Oysters, the Camel Toe Lady Steppers, and the Pussyfooters. I'm just waiting to see who'll take me."

Winter turned as white as his seasonal surname. "Dear God, it's bigger than we thought."

Summer broke into a sweat and clutched his earpiece. "The Vagina has splintered. They're using stolen jewelry to fund multiple terror cells."

The terrorism phrases prompted me to hold up my hand. "Fall

back, Summer and Winter!" I glanced around. I thought I'd get a laugh from that crack, but the bachelorette party was a tougher crowd than the French Quarter revelers who rode out hurricanes drinking Hurricanes at Pat O'Brien's. "I'm a New Orleans PI, and I was talking about Mardi Gras dance troupes, not terrorist groups, you goons."

Winter winced. "You didn't have to call us a name."

Summer sniffed. "That *was* pretty harsh."

*This was the FBI? What did it stand for? Full-Blown Idiots?*

My ringtone went off, and I was glad to have an exit from the conversation. "It's my landlady. She's watching my dog so I'd better take this in the hall."

Merry gave me a curious look, but I avoided her gaze. My landlady was a sixty-something ex-stripper with a *laissez-les-bons-tatas-rouler* look on life, so it was best not to speak to her in public.

"Hey, Glenda. What's up?"

She gave a raucous laugh. "I presume you're surrounded by male strippers, Miss Franki, so you tell me—and make it graphic."

"It isn't that kind of bachelorette party."

"Then it's a funeral."

She didn't know how right she was. "Everything okay with Napoleon?"

"He's randy dandy, sugar. I'm calling because I didn't know what to feed him, so I ran across the street to Thibodeaux's and got him some takeout."

I knew I should've hired a pet sitter. Glenda survived off champagne like vampires did blood, and the only animal she had experience with was a species native to Bourbon Street strip clubs. "I left a note in his bowl that his kibble is in the pantry."

"I looked in the pantry, Miss Franki, but all I could find were bottles of Chianti, a jar of Nutella, and some little brown rocks."

Napoleon and I needed to improve our diets—although

Nutella had milk, hazelnuts, and chocolate, which were all really nutritious. "The rocks are the kibble."

"That's not rat poison?"

"Why would I leave a note about rat poison in my dog's bowl?"

"To keep the rascally rodents from eating his meals, Miss Franki."

The unspoken topic here was that my landlady was unfazed by the notion of me having rats, but I didn't point that out because I was terrified about what my Cairn terrier had eaten. "So what did you give him?"

"Dinner and a show, sugar."

The show part made me pace. Glenda liked to perform for a human-male audience, and because Napoleon once peed on the stem of the giant champagne glass in her living room, we agreed that she'd care for him at my place downstairs. "Could you be more specific?"

"I got him a strip steak, sugar. I always did like the name." She exhaled what was undoubtedly a puff of smoke from her Mae West-style cigarette holder. "As for the show, Philip was training a new bartender who's the spitting image of Mickey Rourke, pre-surgeries. I told him he could slip me a mickey anytime, and I wasn't talking about a drug-laced drink."

*Slip a mickey. Who'd said that earlier?*

Glenda blew out another drag. "So we came back to your place and recreated the infamous scene from *9 1/2 Weeks*, the one where Kim Basinger crawls across the floor, picking up the money he throws at her."

I hadn't seen it, but I could imagine it in my apartment, and I was traumatized. Napoleon was probably still hiding under the zebra chaise longue.

"By sheer coincidence, I was wearing my G pasties and my dollar-bill boa. Anyhow, I never did understand why that scene was so controversial."

She wouldn't, since it depicted how she'd made her living. "I've gotta get back to the party. Just give Napoleon the rocks for breakfast tomorrow...sans the show."

"Funeral pooper."

I smirked and hung up. I'd paced into the lobby where a handcuffed Mo was absorbed in *Weekend at Bernie's II*. Between his TV watching and his eating, he'd given the killer ample opportunity to take and return the room key Babette had left on the reception desk.

*Was Amber working with Mo to steal the bracelet?*

He stuck out his tongue and used it to press the volume button on the remote control.

*Yeah, no.*

He spotted me and straightened. "You need something?"

"Uh, yeah." I leaned on the counter. "I forgot to ask whether any other hotel staff had access to Babette's room tonight. Like a maid?"

He breathed in deep. "Lucinda ain't here in the evenings. Just me and Rock."

"Speaking of Rock, he doesn't have much of a résumé. How'd he get this gig?"

"I referred him. We went to school together."

*Interesting revelation.* "He's not a pickpocket too, is he?"

Mo chuckled. "Nah, he wouldn't wanna risk a hand injury. Even when we was kids, he'd get the girls to carry his books and his cafeteria tray. He's a lucky schmuck like that Charlie."

*And a user like Charlie, too.*

"He's a really good forger, though. I guess because it's a hand skill." Mo lowered his lips to a glass and slurp-licked a sip.

After my stomach stopped churning, I thought of the drug-laced drink Glenda mentioned. I pulled out my phone and googled the expression *slip someone a mickey*. Sure enough, it referred to drugging a drink.

*Zelda.* She accused Kate of slipping Amber a mickey. *Did she know the drinks had been poisoned? If so, was she trying to deflect the blame from herself—or Rock?*

I hurried back to the Big Apple Room. Kate was at the bar next to Babette, whose hair was looking pretty impressive considering it'd been squashed for hours inside the hot dog head-piece. Merry was nearby twirling a fork. "Hey, guys. I'm wondering if we were wrong to focus on the chocolates."

Valentine smoky-eyed Rock, who had his back to us, talking to Zelda at the far end of the bar. "You think it was the drinks?"

Merry threw the fork, which skidded across two tables and then hit the bullseye. "The blade version of rock skimming." She rubbed her hands together for effect. "But yes, injecting a drink would be easier and quicker than the chocolates."

Kate leaned in. "He served Amber two dirty martinis that I saw. And she had at least two more."

I looked at the bar. "True, but I saw Zelda make herself a scotch and soda, so she had access to the alcohol too."

Kate gasped. "I told you she did it. If she thought my Laurie was a boy, then she could've mistaken Amber for Babette."

I blinked. That made no sense given the circumstances, but it did shed some light on the phrase *pregnancy brain.*

Babette bared her teeth. "I don't know, guys. Rock's had it in for me ever since I got the wiener job, but it's hard to imagine him killing me over something so silly. And if I was his intended victim, the weapon couldn't have been a drink because I wasn't here."

"Good point." I massaged my temples. This party was giving *me* pregnancy brain.

"Excuse me for a minute, ladies." Valentine eyed Babette's hair, then swung her long-lashed gaze to a centerpiece on one of the tables. "I need to grab some hair extensions from a candlestick."

*A statement you don't hear at just any bachelorette party.* I took a seat at the bar, where Rock was trying to clean some gunk from the grooves of the bar spill mat.

His brow lowered to Neanderthal level. "Hey, Zelda. Can you get me a toothpick?"

She pulled one from a glass jar right in front of him and handed it to him sideways.

Mo's chuckle echoed in my head. Rock wouldn't even take a toothpick for fear of injuring his precious hands. He had to have a woman take it for him. I gripped the counter.

*That was it! Amber was working with Rock! He had her steal Babette's bracelet!*

I jumped from my stool. "Everyone listen up. It's time to unmask—or maybe I should say *unglove*—the murderer."

Shocked faces turned to the bar, and Rock's model mug turned as hard as his muscles.

"The reason Rock didn't catch Amber when she fell had nothing to do with saving his hands. The truth is, he didn't want to save her. He wanted her dead so he could keep the money he'd get from selling Babette's bracelet all for himself."

Rock raised his gloved hands. "Yo, I didn't kill Amber, and I never heard of no bracelet."

Zelda was so upset, she had to reposition her teeth before she could talk. "Watch what you say about my client, Frenchie, or I'll hit you with a lawsuit."

"What're you gonna do when the police arrest him, Zelda? Sue them, too?"

Merry approached the bar, spinning a fork. "Where are you hiding the bracelet, Rock? You wearing it under that latex?"

"First of all, I don't wear girlie jewelry. And second, have you seen the size of my wrists?" He raised flexed biceps. "They're as big as Schwarzenegger's."

Valentine flailed a hair extension at him. "We wouldn't know because you've been hiding them in those gloves."

"Which are girlie," I added.

Rock went rigid. "The flower-blossom opening provides

maximum coverage. And no way I'd try to steal a sapphire bracelet."

I leaned an arm on the bar. "You would, and you did."

His eyelids lowered. "You got no evidence, lady."

"Actually, I do. Not one person in this room mentioned sapphires—except you."

Rock picked up the soda gun and aimed it at me.

I rolled my eyes. "A guy with a box of rocks for brains has no business in crime."

He threw the gun on the counter and ran.

Kate slid off her stool and gripped her belly. "Someone stop him!"

Valentine grabbed a tub of butterscotch conditioner from the gift table and splattered it on the floor.

Rock slipped and thrashed his arms, causing his gloves to fly off. He screamed in horror, lurched himself forward, and threw his arms behind his back like a dumb jock at a party trying to play Superman. He landed hard on his chest, refusing to catch even himself.

"Valentine! Tie him up with this!" I grabbed the flat iron from her beauty bag and threw it to her.

"That's *your* specialty, Merry." Valentine tossed the flat iron to Merry. The cord twisted in the air and narrowly missed Kate, who ducked and stumbled.

Sensing a disaster of Humpty Dumpty proportions, I threw myself beneath her to break her fall. I watched in slow motion as Kate and the twins came down on my abdomen like a bounce house at a kids' party.

Chelsea and Stanley helped Kate to her feet. Fortunately, she was fine, but I needed a minute. Or a week.

"My hands," Rock yelled. "The circulation is cut off! I could get gangrene!"

I glanced behind me. Valentine and Merry had bound Rock's hands and feet with a flat iron and hair extensions a prettier shade of green than his gloves—and probably my face. "You won't be doing any hand modeling in prison."

"Just latrine duty," Merry said. "With no gloves."

Rock went limp, out like a rock.

I turned my head and saw Zelda hovering over me.

"You hurt, Frenchie?"

I snorted. "What do you think?"

"Serves you right for ratting out my cli—" Her teeth slipped from her mouth and nailed me in the forehead.

*Why didn't I have that cabbie take me back to the airport?*

# VALENTINE

## ARLENE MCFARLANE

*I* left Merry looming over Rock, then grabbed my bag and click-clacked straight for Kate and Franki. "Gee, guys, sorry about the incoming flat iron. That was a close call. Thank goodness, Franki, you've got good reflexes."

"Yours are pretty quick, yourself." Franki grinned, a trace of admiration in her voice.

Kate giggled while patting her belly. "And I'm fine. The last time I had this much attention was when I begged Jim to go to Ben & Jerry's at two a.m. for pickle-flavored ice cream. He would've flown to Timbuktu to keep me from blubbering onto my tummy."

"Pickle-flavored what?" Franki wrinkled her forehead, which was starting to bruise to the shape of Zelda's front incisors.

"I know," Kate answered. "Who can explain preggo woman cravings?"

Not me. I wouldn't even try.

Franki filled us in on Rock's many talents, including that of being a forger. "*That*, of course, came out of Mo's mouth along with mozzarella cheese flecks."

Something about what Franki shared caused goosebumps

down my arms. I backed away on the balls of my feet as gently as if I were passing a sleeping baby. Truth was, the needling that had been bothering me earlier was struggling to surface, and I required a moment to think.

I tiptoed past Agents Summer and Winter who were embroiled in a heated Rock, Paper, Scissors game over extremist groups.

"I *told* you we had to cut loose the whole Monkey Fist thing." Summer threw his hand down in a scissor fashion. "Maybe Agent Spring would be a better partner. At least he listens to what I have to say. And he tells good jokes."

"There you go, undermining me again!" Winter simultaneously made a rock with his fist. "And who ever heard of such a stupid thing? Agents *Spring* and *Summer*! You might as well call yourselves Agents Rain and Sunshine."

I probably wouldn't have been noticed if I'd been driving the Wienermobile, which at this moment was being impounded by the police, pulling into the Park Avenue Hotel lot.

I strode into the hall, details of Amber's murder entrenched in my mind, when there was a tap on my shoulder.

"*Ahhhhh!*" For Pete's sake! I twirled around, ready to fire a handful more of butterscotch conditioners from my bag but stopped short when I came face to face with Detective van der Donk.

He gawked from the conditioners in my hand to my face. "What were you planning to do with those? Untangle my hair?"

I peered up at his graying hair, gave a faint grin, and blew out a sigh. Then I sheepishly shoved the conditioners back in my bag. "A-heh. Sorry."

He smiled, the kind that went right up to his eyes. "Nerves of steel, huh?"

"Something like that."

His voice was understanding, that of a man used to working grueling hours on a police force, a man committed to displaying patience with others. "Good news is we got a call from Niagara Collateral." He wrenched his head toward the street. "Guy there said someone was passing along fake IDs. We knew something was in the works when he mentioned Babette Lang. Seems her name had been forged, and the woman who signed for the bracelet inaccurately signed as Babette Long."

I looked over my shoulder at the party room, recalling what Franki had just shared, then swung my head back to van der Donk. "It comes on good authority that it was Rock who did the forging. He likely did so in order for Amber to pick up the bracelet from the pawnshop."

"Makes sense." He watched as a couple of uniforms hand-cuffed Rock and hauled him to his feet. "Only problem is we don't have the bracelet in question."

At those words, a light bulb the size of a disco ball, which had to be hanging somewhere in this dump, lit up. I hooked my bag over my shoulder and smiled so wide I probably looked like the village idiot. "Come with me."

He gave me a wary eye but silently followed me down the hall into the supply room. "What do you want in here? A mop and pail?"

Without a word, I led him to a shelf at eye level that had a pair of powder blue rubber gloves neatly folded in half. They weren't ordinary cleaning gloves or nitrile hairdressing gloves, and they weren't in a sealed bag like the others. These were a pair of frilly gloves with a flower-blossom opening that was currently hanging over the edge. *This* was what had been needling me earlier. I saw the gloves sitting there when I'd had my run-in with Stanley, but I didn't think much of them at the time. Seemed Rock had backups.

I turned from the shelf to van der Donk and did a Vanna White, hand pose to my find. "Ta-da."

He raised an eyebrow, evidently not into guessing games. "You want gloves to go with the mop and pail?"

I grimaced and gave an internal headshake. But inside I felt myself glowing. This was the missing clue, the part that tied everything together, the pièce de résistance. I reached up, unfolded the frilly pair, and peeked inside the bulkier glove. As expected, the bracelet was there. I slid the delicate jewelry out onto the other glove, the feel of authentic gems wonderfully smooth and cool as it brushed against my palm. "I present to you...the sapphire bracelet."

Van der Donk's face lit up, duly impressed, first time all night I believe—well, except for when Merry hit the bullseye with a dessert fork. "Good work, Miss Valentine. Though you're a little, ahem, impulsive with your beauty tools, your reputation seems accurate." He slipped a pen through the bracelet and nodded with appreciation at not only the crystal-clear sapphires, but the adjoining sparkly diamonds that, in point of fact, took me by surprise.

"Thank you," I said as an afterthought since I was too busy sighing dreamily at the diamonds. Sixteen to be exact, radiant cut, nearly colorless, probably flawless, and at least a half carat per stone. But that was just a humble estimation that I concluded would bring in a hefty five-figure sum in today's market. No wonder Rock wanted to steal Babette's bracelet. Who knew it was this priceless?

"I guess our work here is done." He wrapped the bracelet in his hanky and stuffed it in his pocket. "The guys at the crime lab will want to look at this. But your friend will get it back in due time. I'll make sure of it."

This guy was a straight shooter. Romero would've been lucky to work with him.

We reunited with the other guests who by now had formed small groups and were reviewing the night.

Without further commotion, van der Donk escorted Rock out to the cruiser for his final act, tossing me my flat iron and hair extensions along the way. "You might need these." He winked, keeping his stride, then slowed to a thoughtful halt, jerking his head toward my friends. "You girls make a nifty team. You're like the Four Musketeers."

I grinned and gave a pensive nod. "And to think they started out as three."

"Yeah." He nodded back. "I suppose Dumas rethought that."

I dumped my tools in my bag, rejoined my posse, and shared where we'd found the bracelet. I steadied my gaze on Babette. "At least we now know you weren't the intended murder victim. Target of forgery? Yes. But Rock was more interested in the bracelet than anything."

She knit her eyebrows together. "Then it was Rock who stole the Fentanyl from my bag?"

I shrugged. "Looks like it. He had opportunity, and with everything else going on it was hard to keep track of his whereabouts. But the poison was meant for Amber. He obviously wanted her out of the way so he could keep the bracelet for himself."

Babette went silent as if an unbearable heaviness came over her. "That slimeball. What is it with the male jerks in my world?"

I smoothed a long blonde bang away from her face. "I'm sorry about Charlie, Babette. We were all hoping the night would turn out differently and that he'd be your love match."

Tears brimmed her eyes, but she brushed them away and put on a big smile, the yellows and reds on her hot dog costume adding a glow to her face. "That's okay. What's more important is I've got you friends. Do you know that when I was on my way to the police station tonight, I kept thinking about you guys? Dumbass Charlie was always a burden in my mind."

"He *is* a dumbass," Merry piped.

"Bab-*ette*..." Charlie wailed from the other side of the room. "All I was guilty of was seeing another woman."

Babette stomped over to Charlie, swept the hot dog headpiece off the table where I'd left it, and poised it threateningly at her ex-fiancé. "You lowlife. Not only were you two-timing me, but in the end you're nothing but a classic mooch just like Johnny 'The Mooch' Muccitelli. Plus, you're a bad kisser, you have a drinking problem, *and* you lied about your job. You're not an investment broker or financial advisor or even a bank teller. You're a *stripper*! And not a very good one. You can't even dance!"

Charlie reeled back as if Babette had given him an uppercut to the jaw. He managed to straighten himself and throw a weak smile over his shoulder, but nothing could soften the steely edge in Babette's voice.

"I thought Chelsea introduced Charlie and Babette," Franki whispered. "Somehow I can't see uptight Chelsea in a strip club."

No one answered. We were all too busy watching Babette take charge.

"*This* is how you dance, you moron." She swayed the head-piece seductively in the air and swiveled her hips, singing to Tina Turner's "Private Dancer." Her gyrating was slow and methodical at first, her body in tune to the music. Then she picked up speed, her movements shifting into that of a loose-hipped hula dancer, causing the hot dog to slide down her body.

"Wow." Kate's mouth hung open. "I could never do that in a million years."

"Shh." Merry nudged Kate. "I want to see what happens next."

Babette shimmied out of her costume, not leaving much to the imagination in her push-up bra and spandex briefs.

Charlie gulped as if he'd forgotten how voluptuous she was. "Bab-*ette*..." he wailed, arms out, giving it one last try.

She swung the headpiece over her shoulder like a bat, taking aim, then cut him a stony look. "Get out of here, Charlie Miller, or I'll clock you."

His shoulders sagged, the look on his face morose. It was the end of the road, and Charlie knew it. Without looking back, he trudged out of the hotel and out of Babette's life.

Babette flung the headpiece on the floor by the rest of the

costume, then dusted off her hands, and sashayed over. "Golly, that feels better!"

"Uh, Babette…" Kate stammered. "Do you maybe want to cover yourself with a tablecloth?" She gave a timid smile. "I mean, you look great and all, but you could wrap the material around you like a toga. Just like when we were in college," she added as an incentive.

"*Pff.*" Babette waved Kate's idea away. "I'm done with costumes. Next costume *I* wear will be on Broadway."

Franki smirked. "Brings me back to your night on Bourbon Street when you stripped out of that Mardi Gras Queen number and attempted to switch costumes with the Dat Dog mascot."

A burst of laughter erupted from Merry's lips. "What happened?"

Franki sliced Merry a look. "You don't want to know."

"Those days are done." Babette straightened her back, sending her boobs forward about a foot. "And I won't quit this time until I've made it."

"I like her chutzpah," Merry said, leaning into Kate.

"She has plenty of that," Kate agreed.

"The only thing I don't get about this whole nightmare," Babette said, "is why Rock would risk adding Fentanyl to someone's drink." She pursed her lips, thinking this through. "I mean, he's a bartender. Surely it must've occurred to him that it might not be a bright idea."

Franki snorted. "*Bright* and *Rock* are two words that don't belong in the same sentence."

"On top of which," I said, "often it's the obvious that's overlooked. And everyone *was* focused on the chocolates."

There was a lot of head nodding to that.

"Then who actually told Amber about the party?" Babette asked. "Charlie or Rock?"

I lifted one shoulder. "Hard to say. Amber might've been playing one off the other. Getting what information she could out of Charlie about you and the bracelet, then passing it on to Rock. And since Rock seemed financially hard up, Amber must've taken out her life savings to get the bracelet out of hock. Who knows? Maybe she even told Rock she wanted to quit the whole scheme and make it work with Charlie. All good reasons for Rock to get rid of her and pocket the bracelet for himself."

Babette quivered from head to toe and vented a huge sigh. "I'm just glad Grandma Barbie's heirloom will be back with its rightful owner."

Merry grinned. "*I'm* just glad Valentine passed it on to van der Donk and not Abbott and Costello from the FBI. They'd still be playing Rock, Paper, Scissors, trying to figure out what to do with it."

"They weren't so bad," Babette cooed, the lines around her eyes drawn back in delight.

I slipped away to get Babette's bag from my room, then presented it and all the goodies inside after the other guests vacated the place.

"A new bag! And hot pink! Guys, you shouldn't have." She embraced the purse to her bosom like a long-lost friend, smiling at each of us. "But I'm glad you did. Thank you!"

"Uh…" Franki gestured to the bag. "Valentine was the one—"

"—who picked out the color," I finished, winking at Franki.

There was no need to correct Babette. Van der Donk was right. We *were* like the Four Musketeers. *All for one and one for all.*

I warmed inside. I liked the sound of that.

The five of us sat with our feet up—Babette in her new furry stiletto slippers—sipping drinks, eating cake, and poking Dora the Explorer balloons floating at waist-level. There was contentment among friends in the air and a calmness that spoke to me like a rich vanilla scent. Wait. My lipstick was vanilla-scented. Maybe that was what I was smelling. *No.* This was definitely the cozy aroma of friends bonding.

Babette rummaged through the bag, gushing. "Massage oils,

bubble bath, and *red jelly beans*! My favorite." She plopped some in each of our drinks. "They go great with mai tais."

Nobody was drinking mai tais since our one and only bartender had been dragged away in handcuffs, but the Shirley Temples were a close second—at least for Kate and me. Franki and Merry had commandeered the bar and were experimenting with liqueurs I'd never heard of.

"There was also a bottle of champagne," I confessed. "But Stanley was the receiver of that gift."

Babette puckered her lips. "That little dweeb. Never mind me owing on the hot dog costume. I should make *him* pay for taking my gift."

I grinned inside. "I think he paid enough."

She hopped off her chair in her sexy slippers and bustled us all together into a circle, squishing me against her on one side in my pink dress—oh what the heck, it did look like a tutu—while squashing pregnant Kate on the other. With Franki in black down to her slick boots and happy-go-lucky Merry rounding off our circle, I was sure we were a sight to behold.

Babette proudly met each of us eye to eye. "Thank heavens for you guys, solving this case. You make a killer foursome. And now that *I'm* here we're the Fabsome Five. I came up with that on my own. Don't you love it?"

We all nodded yes and, in truth, if it hadn't been for Babette, I never would've met these incredible women.

"This is the best bachelorette party I've ever been to...and I've been to a few," she declared. "Balloons, cake, and good friends. What more could I ask for?"

There was a slight movement at the entrance, and we all swiveled our heads to see who was crashing our party. A frumpy-looking man, about sixty, 5'10", in a worn shirt and tattered jeans raised his hands palms out in a *Sorry to interrupt* motion.

"May I help you?" I asked, breaking loose from our circle of supersleuths.

"Uh, yeah. I'm Harry." His tone was apologetic, his words hesitant. "There was a mix-up at Higgly Piggly today, and I think you got my cake."

I pivoted to the others, eyes wide, and signaled to the cake that was half gone.

Leave it to Babette. In a throaty, sensual voice, she broke out singing "Happy Birthday to You."

We all joined in, and Harry beamed like he'd been promoted from servanthood to king, bobbing his head merrily in time to the tune.

"Here! Have some cake." Kate held up a plate with a piece that said *APPY IRTH*.

"Thanks." Relief flooded his voice. "You wouldn't believe the crazy day I've had."

Babette walked him arm in arm to the table. "Honey…" She patted his sleeve and stepped over the hot dog costume crumpled on the floor. "Have I got a story for *you*."

# EPILOGUE: KATE

## DIANA ORGAIN

 o Do:

1. Introduce Babette to Vincente Domingo.
2. Keep in touch with Valentine, Franki, and Merry.
3. Laurie's first birthday is quickly approaching! 💀
4. Invites, party theme, location?
5. Get a massage. Really.

I STRETCHED my feet on the ottoman so Jim could reach them while ignoring Whiskers meowing. For the moment, I was content in life, snuggling Laurie on my lap while Jim rubbed my feet.

"Honey, we missed you so much, but I'm proud of you. There's no way we could've let Babette marry a guy like Charlie." He pressed his thumb into my arch.

"I know, right?" I inhaled Laurie's baby scent into my heart. "I missed you guys so much I thought I'd implode. On the flight home, I literally calculated the number of seconds before I could hold you and Laurie. I don't know what I missed more, Laurie's powder-fresh scent or your supersonic thumb.

Jim smiled then pressed his thumb into the ball of my foot.

I laughed. "Okay. It was you I missed more."

He chuckled. "Liar."

I slipped my feet out of his hands and planted a kiss on his lips. We cuddled Laurie, now asleep, between us.

"Jim, her first birthday is coming up."

"Yeah. Your mom told me she wanted to go with an Avengers theme for the party."

I laughed so hard I woke Laurie, who only reached out a chubby hand to my cheek and mumbled a sleepy "Mama."

"I hope you told Mom no," I whispered.

Jim flashed me a wicked grin. "I told her to go for it."

"I'll call her in the morning."

"You should call her now and let her know you got home safe."

I nodded, sinking into the couch. Jim removed Laurie from my arms. "You want me to call her?"

Whiskers jumped to my now free lap and purred furiously. I rubbed her ears.

"Yes," I whispered, my eyelids heavy.

*Flying cross-country while pregnant with twins after solving a murder was no joke.*

"Tell her I'm home safe, and tomorrow I'll plan the party. Definitely no Avengers, and while you're at it, tell her no clowns. Not even Vicente." I laughed at my own joke.

Vicente was a local PI who was a friend, but also a thorn in my side and probably my biggest competition in the PI business.

"You can't keep Vicente from the party," Jim said.

"I was thinking of setting him up with Babette."

His eyes widened. "What?"

"She wants to move to New York, audition like mad for Broadway. Take the thing super seriously, and you know she's got the voice. She can sing, dance, and act. She's a triple threat. I always told her that. She should do it. *Carpe diem*, you know."

Jim snuggled Laurie. "I always support ladies carpe-ing the diem, but what does Vicente have to do with it?"

I chuckled. "Charlie was bad for her. Vicente wants to go to New York, doesn't he?"

Jim frowned. "Does he?"

Vicente was also a budding playwright. This matchmaking wasn't coming from a place of malice. I really thought Vicente and Babette could hit it off.

Jim left the living room to put Laurie down in the crib. I folded my feet under me as I stroked the cat.

"I think they'd like each other," I called to Jim. He returned to the room, and I continued. "I mean, Vicente's a playwright, Babette an actress…"

"You got to do better than that," Jim said. "What are you saying? Babette needs Vicente to make it on Broadway?"

"No!" I feigned outrage. "Maybe *he* needs *her*."

Jim smiled and pulled me into an embrace. "Well, *I* need *you*. Don't leave me again, okay? At least not for a while."

I pressed my lips to his, love warming my heart. "I promise, even though my trip was incredible and I met some new besties, I'm not leaving you again until these twins are born."

"Darn right." His chest puffed with satisfaction. "Between Whiskers, Laurie, me, and your mom, you got all the adventure you can handle right here."

I smiled and sank deeper into his strong arms. "There's no place like home, honey."

# EPILOGUE: MERRY

## LESLIE LANGTRY

*I*t was a long flight home. Well, not as long as the time I flew Aeroflot across the entirety of Russia dressed as a banana with a flash drive of Russian missile defenses duct-taped to my inner thigh, but long nonetheless. I awoke to see the little old lady sitting next to me holding her knitting needles defensively. She said I was mumbling something in my sleep about Kim Jong-un wearing assless chaps and a killer hand model. She never really relaxed until we landed in Des Moines. I'm pretty sure I could've taken her.

Rex texted that he couldn't come for me due to a situation in the break room involving Officer Kevin Dooley—town paste eater—and two vending machines. Typical. But I did wonder who he'd sent in his place.

"There she is!" Hilly shouted on the other side of security, jumping up and down like a kid who'd just mainlined a box of Pixy Stix.

Betty just stood there next to her, studying my every move. Interesting how the adult assassin was acting more like a kid than the little girl.

"Thanks for picking me up," I said as I joined them and Hilly crushed me in a bear hug. "I guess Rex had an emergency or something."

"Oh, that." Hilly waved me off. "I did that. I just wanted to pick you up myself."

"She handcuffed Dooley inside the machines," Betty said. "It was pretty impressive."

"You handcuffed him *inside* the machines?" I had to ask. "How did you do that?"

"Just one hand to the inner workings of each machine." Hilly smirked. "Child's play really. So, how did it go?"

As tempted as I was to grill them on what was going on with my garage, I instead filled them in on my adventures as we collected my suitcase and during the half-hour drive home from Des Moines.

"A disappearance *and* a poisoning?" Betty grumped. "I miss all the cool stuff."

"And I met these really awesome women," I said, ignoring her complaint. I told them how Valentine uses styling supplies to catch bad guys, how Kate is exceptional at getting folks to talk, and how Franki can read people like nobody's business. They'd all be excellent spies.

Hilly's face fell like it did whenever she thought someone was more of my bestie than she was. Considering the damage she'd done to my old house and the possibility of me ever getting insurance again, I let her mope.

After we pulled into our driveway, I jumped out to look across the street at my old house.

*How...? Is that...?*

"A two-story garage?" I shouted as I ran over to it. "What am I going to do with a two-story garage?"

The top story looked like a castle with two open-gauge towers on either side, in addition to some unusual modifications.

"Are those machine gun embrasures?" My jaw dropped.

Betty gave me that look she often did when she thought I was an idiot. "Of course! How can you fight off an angry mob without machine guns?"

I pointed at one of the towers. "Why are there arrow slits?"

Hilly stared at me. "What if there's an apocalypse and we don't have access to ammo?"

"Girl Scouts are supposed to be prepared," Betty added. "Did you fall into Niagara Falls and hit your head?"

"No." But now I had the startling realization that with all the madness at that hellhole hotel, I never did get to visit the Falls. Huh.

Hilly slapped me a little too hard on the back. "We added Dora the Explorer curtains and a wine-and-cheesecake fridge."

"Why didn't you lead with that?" I stared at the monstrosity with new eyes. "Okay. I approve."

"We replaced your garage door with a portcullis." Hilly pulled a remote out and hit a button. The portcullis dropped quickly, almost cutting a worker in half. He rolled away out of danger and gave us a startled look.

"I just don't get it." I walked over and touched the gate. "How did you get the city to agree to this?"

Hilly shrugged. "We got a license to crenellate."

I turned to her. "Who's There has a license to crenellate? Kings of England used those in the Middle Ages to grant permission to nobles to fortify their castles!"

How did I know that? I once had to impersonate a medieval academic at a conference in Turkmenistan. Unfortunately, I didn't realize I'd be presenting on the subject of weaponizing castles until I was called forth out of the audience to do so. Fortunately, Riley used the hidden mic in my ear to read the Wikipedia entry on the subject or I'd have made a break for it. Little-known fact—there are countries where you can do jail time for impersonating a historian.

Betty nodded. "Hilly talked them into it. She's kind of scary. Want a tour?"

I walked back and looked at the castle-like garage. "This is pretty cool, but I'm not sure my insurance will cover this."

Hilly cocked her head to one side. "The insurance guy has vanished. I can find him if you want. Shouldn't take long. I put a tracker on his car…just in case."

"No, thanks," I insisted. "I'm good."

TEN MINUTES LATER, as we sat on the roof of the castle, eating cheesecake and drinking wine (Betty had sparkling juice), I had to admit, these two had outdone themselves. What I didn't tell them was that in a week or so, I'd hire different contractors to take this down and return it to its original state. The castle thing didn't really work with the aesthetic of a one-story ranch-style house.

I was keeping the fully stocked wine-and-cheesecake fridge, though. There was no way I was parting with that. I texted a selfie of me with it to my new friends with the message, *This is what awaits you if you ever come to my hometown.* There wasn't much that would entice them to leave Boston, New Orleans, or San Francisco for this little town in the middle of nowhere. We didn't have tons of interesting history, stunning architecture, or a lot of fun things to do.

But at least we didn't have bartenders who wanted to be hand models. And there was satisfaction in that.

# EPILOGUE: FRANKI

## TRACI ANDRIGHETTI

"*H*ome, sweet home." My best friend and boss, Veronica Maggio, patted me in the passenger seat as she pulled her Mercedes into the driveway of the dilapidated fourplex in Uptown, where we rented adjacent apartments from Glenda.

*'Home, sour home' was more fitting.* I stared out the car window at the graveyard across the street, and a gargoyle atop a crypt stared back. "After the Park Avenue Hotel, the cemetery seems almost welcoming."

Veronica removed Prada sunglasses the same shade of blue as her eyes and shook out her blonde locks. "I feel so bad for both of the women involved, but Babette's lucky to have had you four sleuths on the case. Since she came back to the hotel during the party without telling anyone, she could've taken the fall for killing Amber."

"Yeah, I suspected her myself."

She snorted. "You suspect everyone, Franki."

"And with good reason." I pushed open the car door a tad testily. "You never know what people are capable of, especially when they have a cheating fiancé and a suitcase full of drugs at their disposal."

Veronica shrugged. "Which is what keeps us in business."

I climbed from the car and grabbed my suitcase from the backseat. "You wanna come in? I've got Chianti, Nutella, and kibble."

Her head retracted. "As tempting as that sounds, I can't. I'm meeting a client at Private Chicks in twenty minutes."

"Please tell me it's not a homicide case."

She slid her Pradas back on. "No can do. She was reluctant to give me any details over the phone."

"Fingers crossed it's just another cheating spouse case—without a murder." I slammed the car door and dragged my suitcase up the driveway as Veronica drove away.

When I entered my living room, I wondered why I'd been in such a hurry to come home. I'd been renting the apartment from Glenda for over two years, and yet the décor was still a shock. There was no getting used to French Bordello Funeral Parlor.

My Cairn terrier, Napoleon, eyed me from the zebra chaise longue—belly up, legs splayed. *Did Glenda feed him oysters for breakfast?*

His tacky pose reminded me that before I unpacked, I had urgent business to attend to, i.e., scour my place for evidence of the Glenda and Mickey Rourke-lookalike show—a G pastie, a stray dollar bill—and promptly remove it with gloves à la Rock Stone. I didn't find anything, but the eyes on the bear skin rug looked a little more glazed than usual.

I pulled my suitcase into the bedroom. As I unzipped it, a pharmacy worth of medicine fell out. "*Mannaggia.* Babette and I switched suitcases in the lobby."

A sad sigh escaped my lips. I wasn't thrilled about contacting her so soon after what happened, not to mention dealing with the shipping. But on the positive side, I now had plenty of pain reliever, which would come in handy. Because I was pretty sure Zelda's teeth had cracked my skull.

The sound of metal dragging across linoleum brought me to the kitchen, where Napoleon hovered over his bowl, demanding dinner. I poured him some kibble.

His Brindle head lowered to the little brown rocks, then he raised brown eyes that accused me of trying to poison him.

My eyes went feline. "If you want strip steak, you'll have to take it up with Glenda."

He picked up a piece of kibble and stared at me while chewing it slowly.

Fortunately, the dog didn't have opposable thumbs. If he did, he might try to inject me with Babette's Fentanyl.

My ringtone sounded from the bedroom.

"Probably Babette calling about her suitcase." I went to the bed and looked at my phone. Happiness warmed my chest. It was my fiancé, Bradley, who was the polar opposite of Charlie Miller.

"Hey, honey," I answered, wishing he hadn't left on a business trip the day I'd returned. "How was your flight?"

"Make that plural." His tone was tense. "The New Orleans flight got diverted to Buffalo because of weather, then we had an unruly passenger on the flight to Boston. The guy was so out of control that the captain came on the speaker and asked all strong males to come to the front of the aircraft to help."

"That's terrible." I sank onto the fuchsia duvet, also courtesy of my landlady. "What set him off?"

"Probably booze, but who knows."

"You're a big, strong guy," I said in a husky voice. "Did you take him down yourself?"

He chuckled. "Didn't have to. A woman traipsed down the aisle with some type of flat curling iron and tied him up."

*Valentine?*

"Anyway, babe, I need to run and catch a cab. I was just calling to make sure you got home safe and let you know that someone will be staying at my place while I'm gone. She's my mother's goddaughter from here in Boston."

*The same way I'd met Babette last Mardi Gras.*

"While we're on the subject, I doubt she'll need anything, but if she does, could you be available?"

I flashed back to picking up bombed Babette at New Orleans Central Lockup, the Dat Dog costume in my convertible, and the whole sordid saga of the Big Apple Room bachelorette party.

Then I got a vivid visual of the mozzarella in Mo's teeth.

"Ugh, I'm sorry, Bradley. Veronica and I just got a new homicide case, so I have to work."

# EPILOGUE: VALENTINE

## ARLENE MCFARLANE

"*D*id Phyllis ever finish perming Mrs. Horowitz's hair?" I asked Max on speakerphone on the drive home from Boston Logan Airport.

"We can talk about it another day." Max's way of evading the question.

"Oh boy. Should I brace myself or ram my car into a guardrail right now?"

"No need to get cranky, lovey."

If there was anything that put me on high alert it was when Max told me not to get cranky *and* pretend everything was okay. "Just tell me already. What happened?"

"Fine. If you must know. Jock stepped in after the spider incident, turned Mrs. Horowitz into Zsa Zsa Gabor, and calmed Phyllis down better than if I'd stuck a sock in her yap."

I pictured Jock's hulking muscles and gorgeous smile and had no doubt he'd done as Max had said. Jock was so persuasive he could make a snail uncurl and surrender.

"Mind you," Max went on, "it took the rest of the afternoon to clean Phyllis's mess, but that's a horror story for another time. Aren't you glad you took the weekend off?"

"Yeah, it was a real holiday." No sarcasm there. No siree.

I said bye to Max and pulled into my driveway, happy to be home, yet missing my new friends. My mind suddenly shifted from my eventful weekend to the silver pickup parked in front of my house.

Uh-oh. Romero.

I slid my gaze from his truck to my front porch and swallowed hard. Last time Romero had waited for me on my front porch we'd had words. Well, I wasn't going to be intimidated by a six-foot, macho, hard-headed cop. I'd done nothing wrong. Okay, maybe I'd become involved in a little homicide, something he wouldn't be too crazy about. *That* could've happened to anyone.

I set my shoulders back, fluffed my hair, and lugged my stuff up the front steps. I tried not to stare at how dark and handsome Romero looked in the dim light from the street, but it was tough to ignore how virile he was. The broad shoulders and constant five o'clock shadow got me every time.

Romero assessed me slowly from head to toe, his gaze penetrating. He leaned back on my porch chair, his feet up on what looked like a piece of my luggage. "Some guy dropped this off." He gave a slight nod to the bag. "Said the airline sends their apologies for not delivering 'Miss Beaumont's party bag' to New York."

Right. Dumb suitcase never did make it to the hotel.

He swung his feet to the ground and strolled over, not taking his eyes off me. "Welcome home." He wrapped his arms around the small of my back, his masculine Arctic Spruce scent sending tingles down my spine as he drew me in.

I gulped and peered up at him, my heart pounding from his strong presence and warm embrace.

After a hot kiss that told me in no uncertain terms just how much Romero missed me, he took my keys, opened the door, and followed me into the house, dragging my luggage behind. "What do you want to tell me about first? The party, the missing bachelorette, or the murder."

Barely pulling myself together after that passionate kiss, I flopped my bag on the kitchen counter and whirled around. "I was only gone a few days. What makes you think there was a murder?"

He angled back against the counter and folded his arms across his toned chest. "I left the NYPD to work here. I didn't fall off the face of the earth."

*Van der Donk.* "Sheesh, is nothing sacred?"

"What do you expect? It's not every day a cop—or *anyone*—meets a gutsy beautician who doubles her beauty tools as weapons *and* sets out to seek justice."

I faked indignance. "If you must know, I had no plans to use my weapons—I mean tools—this weekend. It sort of just…happened."

His manner was unbending. "Like how you once also *happened* to nearly blind a felon by firing an elastic band in his eye."

I slung my hands on my hips with a *humph.* "He had it coming." And that was all I was going to say on the subject.

"Or the time you drove an ornamental chopstick from your hair into a felon's clavicle bone."

"If you mean the collar bone, just say so. And for your information, that killer had it coming as well. Now if you're done listing the ways I catch criminals, you can stuff your badge back in your pocket and march right out the door. I'm a little busy getting my life back on track to listen to any more criticisms."

My phone—which had slid from my bag onto the counter—pinged. I ignored it due to the fact that Romero hooked his arm around my waist and thudded me tightly against his body.

"You're awfully saucy." His voice was low with desire. "I might have to tame that attitude with something more…intimate."

Oh boy. Was it hot in here? It felt scorching, and the predatory look in Romero's eyes made me hotter because there was promise in those eyes, enough to melt any woman—saucy, gutsy, or otherwise.

"Well?" The cheeky expression I wore belied the yearning inside. "What are you waiting for? I haven't got all night."

*Ping.*

Romero didn't buy the act. Furthermore, he wasn't one to be distracted by a pinging phone when he had other things on his mind. He took his finger and tilted up my chin, forcing me to see the hunger in his eyes. "We've got nothing *but* all night."

He planted a seductive kiss on my lips, trailing his mouth to my neck, then my shoulder. "In fact…" His sexy gaze roamed to my luggage, a wicked grin creeping up his face. "…let's start by seeing what's in that party bag."

My phone pinged for a third time and, unlike Romero, it was killing me not to look at it. I pushed him in the direction of my suitcase and swept my phone off the counter.

I scrolled like mad down our group chat we'd newly renamed *4 Sleuths*, eyes wide at the selfie Merry had taken of herself with her new wine-and-cheesecake fridge. I sighed with pleasure. It would be nice to see these girls again under better circumstances.

A link suddenly popped up from Franki to an upcoming hair show in New Orleans. *Valentine, saw this…thought of you! When can you get here? Actually, what's everyone's schedules like? We could make it a reunion.*

I glanced over my shoulder at Romero dragging my suitcase into the bedroom. Then I centered back on my phone. I took a second to think of a response, then tapped away, unable to control the grin from sliding up my face.

# BEHIND THE BOOK

As ideas often go, this one came to me on an early morning walk, when I usually plot my books. This particular morning, my mind took a detour from my series to ask this question: What if four heroines joined in solving a mystery? Not just any heroines or any mystery. But four diverse protagonists, each with their own series, teaming together to make a hilarious, entertaining whodunit, much like a superhero movie that includes crossovers between characters and stories.

The idea fleshed itself out in the coming days. Next was to find three authors with great comedic voices, their own cozy series, and an array of eager fans. I didn't need to look far. Leslie Langtry, Diana Orgain, and Traci Andrighetti were witty authors whom I already respected and admired. They were excited about this prospect and agreed that our first-person narratives and our heroines' special skill sets would blend well together in forming an unstoppable force. In short, we felt this series would be unique.

We created LMAO Press, an acronym representing our last names, and a dazzling cover, and knew *4 Sleuths* was meant to be.

I hope you enjoy the series as much as we enjoy writing it!

Arlene ~

# PREORDER BOOK 2 NOW!

The killer foursome will be back for a second mystery in *4 Sleuths & A Burlesque Dancer*!

After a murderous bachelorette party in Niagara Falls, Valentine, Merry, Kate, and Franki decide it's time to relax and have some fun in the Big Easy. New Orleans turns out to be anything but easy when the killer foursome stumble across the body of a formerly famous, elderly Dolphin burlesque dancer. To make matters worse, NOLA's finest arrest Kate's husband Jim as the prime suspect!

The four sleuths jump into action to catch the killer in a race against time that takes them to the seedier side of the French Quarter where they tussle with strippers, mud wrestlers, and dubious all-you-can-eat crawfish buffets.

Between cranky Cajuns, mysterious Spanish dignitaries, and a bizarre running of the bulls, these four sleuths don't have time to Let the Good Times Roll before Jim takes the fall for the Dolphin dancer's murder!

Get reacquainted with:

Valentine Beaumont ~ Boston sleuth and gutsy beautician

Kate Connolly ~ San Francisco part-time crime-solver and sleep-deprived new mom

Merry Wrath ~ Iowa ex-CIA operative turned Girl Scout leader

Franki Amato ~ New Orleans PI and victim of a serial-matchmaking Sicilian nonna

...and help them solve this crime!

While you're waiting for *4 Sleuths & A Burlesque Dancer*, catch up on the adventures of each heroine in her own series.

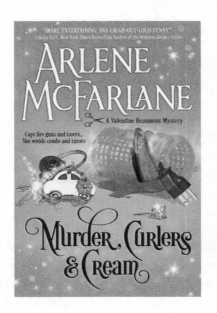

**Valentine:**

Arlene McFarlane is the *USA Today* bestselling author of the Murder, Curlers series. She's won and placed in over 30 contests, including the Readers' Favorite Book Awards, the Golden Heart®, the Daphne du Maurier, and the Chanticleer International Mystery & Mayhem Book Awards. She's also received a Voice Arts nomination for her audiobook, Murder, Curlers & Cream. Previously an aesthetician, Arlene still dabbles in the beauty industry. She's also an accomplished pianist. When time allows, she plays publicly and posts makeovers on her website. Visit arlenemcfarlane.com/ to learn more!

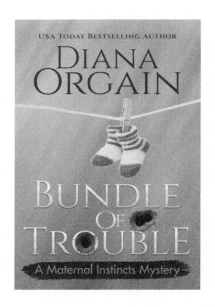

**Kate**:

Diana Orgain is the *USA Today* bestselling author of the Maternal Instincts Mystery Series. She is also the Author of the Love or Money Mystery series and The Roundup Crew Mysteries (Yappy Hour and Trigger Yappy). Diana is the *New York Times* Bestselling co-author of the Scrapbooking Mystery Series with Laura Childs. To keep up to date with the latest releases visit Diana at dianaorgain.com/.

**Merry**:

Leslie Langtry is the *USA Today* bestselling author of the Merry Wrath Cozy Comedy series (Merit Badge Murder), the Ukulele Mysteries (Ukulele Murder) and the Greatest Hits dark comedy series—now in development for a TV series ('Scuse Me While I Kill This Guy). Stop by leslielangtry.com/ to find out more!

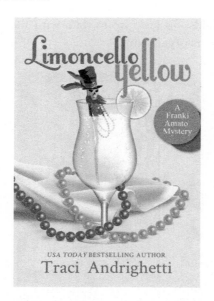

**Franki:**

Traci Andrighetti is the *USA Today* bestselling author of the Franki Amato mysteries and the Danger Cove Hair Salon mysteries. In her previous life, she was an award-winning literary translator and a Lecturer of Italian at the University of Texas at Austin, where she earned a PhD in Applied Linguistics. But then she got wise and ditched that academic stuff for a life of crime—writing, that is. Get news of Traci's upcoming books and latest capers at traciandrighetti.com.

Made in the USA
Monee, IL
30 July 2022

10537217R00125